SILENT
SUPERSTITIONS

Christy of Cutter Gap

SILENT
SUPERSTITIONS

THE SERIES

Based on the novel Christy *by*

CATHERINE MARSHALL

EVERGREEN
— FARM —

an imprint of
GILEAD PUBLISHING

Silent Superstitions: The Christy® of Cutter Gap series
Adapted by C. Archer
Copyright © 1995 by Marshall-LeSourd, LLC

Published by Evergreen Farm, an imprint of Gilead Publishing, LLC,
Wheaton, Illinois, USA.
www.gileadpublishing.com/evergreenfarm

This is a work of fiction. Names, characters, places, and incidents are products of the author's imagination or are used fictitiously. Any similarity to actual people, organizations, and/or events is purely coincidental.

ISBN: 978-1-68370-159-0 (printed softcover)
ISBN: 978-1-68370-160-6 (ebook)

Cover design by Larry Taylor
Cover illustrations © Larry Taylor. All rights reserved.
Interior design by Beth Shagene
Ebook production by Book Genesis, Inc.

Printed in the United States of America.

18 19 20 21 22 23 24 / 5 4 3 2 1

The Characters

Christy Rudd Huddleston, a nineteen-year-old girl

Christy's students:
   Rob Allen, fourteen
   Creed Allen, nine
   Bessie Coburn, twelve
   Wraight Holt, seventeen
   Zacharias Holt, nine
   Becky Holt, seven
   Vella Holt, five
   Isaak McHone, twelve
   Smith O'Teale, fifteen
   Orter Ball O'Teale, eleven
   Mountie O'Teale, ten
   George O'Teale, nine
   Mary O'Teale, eight
   Thomas O'Teale, six
   Ruby May Morrison, thirteen
   John Spencer, fifteen
   Clara Spencer, twelve
   Zady Spencer, ten
   Lundy Taylor, seventeen

Alice Henderson, a Quaker mission worker from Ardmore, Pennsylvania

Granny O'Teale, great-grandmother of the O'Teale children

Swannie O'Teale, a mountain woman

Nathan O'Teale, her husband
(Parents of Christy's students Smith, Orter Ball, Mountie, George, Mary, and Thomas)

Wilmer O'Teale, the epileptic O'Teale son

David Grantland, the young minister

Ida Grantland, David's sister

Dr. Neill MacNeill, the physician of the Cove

Jeb Spencer, a mountain man

Fairlight Spencer, his wife
(Parents of Christy's students John, Clara, Zady)

One

"She's a witch, I tell you! Ugly as a coot with hardly no hair. She's got monstrous red eyes and fingernails like the claws of a hawk!" Mary O'Teale paused to warm her hands by the pot-bellied stove in the one-room schoolhouse.

Her listeners crowded closer.

"Old Marthy's her name," she continued, lowering her voice to a whisper. "Late at night when the moon's as full as a pumpkin, she comes 'round, makin' mischief. If she takes a dislikin' to you, she'll sneak inside while you're a-dreamin' and put a curse on you."

As she listened from her desk, Christy Huddleston couldn't help smiling. Eight-year-old Mary definitely had a vivid imagination. Christy knew her students loved to tell each other "haunt tales." But she worried about the younger children. They were easily frightened, and she didn't want the stories getting out of hand.

"You're just talkin' to hear yerself talk, Mary," said Ruby Mae Morrison, a thirteen-year-old with vibrant red hair and a personality to match. "Ain't nobody ever seen Old Marthy."

Mary jutted her chin. "My great granny has," she replied. She inched her right foot closer to the old stove. Like most of the children at the mission school, she did not own a pair of shoes. Even now, in January, Mary and her friends walked to school barefoot.

Ruby Mae twisted a strand of hair around her index finger. "You're sayin' Granny's seen a witch, up close-like?"

Mary nodded. "Granny saw Old Marthy make someone eat a witch ball."

"What's—what's that?" asked Ruby Mae.

"A witch ball's a bunch of pine needles, all wrapped 'round and 'round with a person's hair."

"What happens when you eat it?"

"At the strike of twelve," Mary whispered, "you turn into a big, hairy old bat. And there ain't no turnin' back, neither!"

Christy cleared her throat. "You know, it's almost time for school to start," she said, giving Mary a patient smile. "Maybe we've had enough of these silly stories for one day."

"But Teacher, they ain't silly," Mary said. "They're haunt tales."

"Girls," Christy said gently, "are any of you afraid of these scary stories?"

No one answered.

"Well, let me ask you this. Are any of you afraid of the dark?"

Vella Holt, a tiny five-year-old with auburn pigtails, climbed onto Christy's lap. "Oh, yes'm, it's scary to have to leave the firelight and walk into the shadows to bed. Most nights, I put the covers over my head."

"Children!" Ruby Mae scoffed.

Christy couldn't help grinning. Christy knew for a fact that Ruby Mae still liked to sleep with a tattered rag doll.

"It gives me prickles to peer at the dark," Vella whispered to Christy. "I'm always scared for fear I'll see a ghost."

"I'll let you in on a little secret," Christy said. "I was like that when I was a girl."

"You was?" Mary exclaimed.

"I'd lie there in my bed, shivering and shaking, thinking of all the stories I'd heard about ghosts and witches and whatnot."

"So how'd you get over it?" Ruby Mae asked.

"One day they sang a certain song at Sunday school. Seemed as if it was just for me. I'll sing it for you—

> *"God will take care of you*
> *Through every day, o'er all the way,*
> *He will take care of you,*
> *He will take care of you."*

Mary nodded thoughtfully. "That's right nice. I like the sound of it."

"So whenever I was scared of the dark," Christy continued, stroking little Vella's hair, "I'd sing those four lines over and over to myself. And you know what, girls? After a while, the love of God was more real to me than any old ghost. Pretty soon all the ghosts went away. Ever since then, the dark has seemed friendly and cozy."

Mary reached over and gave her a shy hug. "Sing it again, Teacher, will you? Then I won't disremember it."

As Christy repeated the song, more of her students rushed into the schoolroom that also served as a church. She watched them as they entered—ragged, pale, probably hungry, almost always dirty. And as she sang, she was reminded once again of the beauty in those eager faces, and that the task set before her was a huge and difficult one.

When Christy had arrived here just a little over a week ago, she'd been full of high hopes about her new job as a teacher at the mission school in Cutter Gap, Tennessee. She'd never dreamed her class would contain sixty-seven students ranging in age from five to seventeen. She'd never imagined that she'd be teaching in such primitive conditions, with just a handful of worn books and an assortment of borrowed, battered desks. A few of her students had basic arithmetic and reading skills, but most had never set foot in a schoolroom before.

Christy finished the song, but Mary and the others kept singing it over and over. Teaching school in Cutter Gap wasn't going to be an easy job. Christy had quickly discovered this during her first long week at the mission school. But as she listened to Mary and the others raise their voices in song, she had the feeling it might just turn out to be more rewarding than she'd ever hoped.

⟵#⟶

That noon, Mary and her older sister, Mountie, slowly climbed up the steep hill behind the school. The dinner spell—Teacher called it "noon recess"—was almost over. But Mary wanted to get a look at the new ice slide the big boys had made.

After the last snowstorm, the boys had created a long, narrow trail by packing down the snow. They'd drenched it with buckets of water, then let the slide freeze. Everyone agreed it was the best sliding hill anyone had seen in a long time.

Mary clutched Mountie's hand when they reached the top of the slide. Several of the older boys were lined up, waiting to belly flop down the icy chute. Some of them were using an old rag rug for a sled.

"Chicken."

Mary cringed when she heard the familiar voice. She turned to see Lundy Taylor approaching.

"We ain't chicken," Mary replied. She squeezed her big sister's hand a little tighter. "We just don't want to."

"Don't want to 'cause you're chicken," Lundy said with a sneer.

Mary watched as her big brother, Smith, sped down the steep icy path. He slowed to a stop at the edge of the schoolyard.

"Besides, Teacher said only the big boys could go," Mary said.

"So how's come you're up here?" Lundy demanded. "You and Mush-mouth?"

Mary stared up at the big boy looming above her. Lundy was seventeen and she was only eight, which was bad enough. It didn't help that he was the biggest bully in the state of Tennessee, maybe even in the world. It was too bad Lundy and her brother were friends. Still, she had to stand up for her big sister. People were always picking on Mountie because she couldn't talk like everyone else.

"Don't you go callin' Mountie names," Mary said. She put her arm around Mountie's thin shoulders. Mountie was two years older than Mary but needed a lot of protecting.

A bell clanged loudly.

Mary looked down to see the new teacher on the porch,

ringing the bell. She was so beautiful! After four days of school, Mary still couldn't get over it. Maybe it was because Teacher came from a big city. Or maybe it was her fancy clothes—shoes of real leather and a red sweater so soft you could melt for the feel of it.

But Mary was pretty sure there was something else that made Teacher so beautiful. It was her eyes, wide and blue as a June sky. Every time Mary looked into those eyes, she felt safe and warm, the way she felt all wrapped up in one of her granny's quilts. Those were magic eyes. Pure magic.

The bell clanged again.

"The dinner spell's over," Mary said.

Lundy held up a hand. "Not for Mush-mouth, it ain't."

Mary could hear trouble in his voice, but by the time she yanked on Mountie's arm, Lundy's strong hands had already clamped onto her sister's shoulders.

Mountie's eyes were bright with fear.

"Let her go, Lundy!" Mary cried. "You're hurtin' her!"

"Whatever you say," Lundy said, shoving Mountie aside.

Mary grabbed Mountie and turned to leave, but suddenly Lundy's big foot was in the way. Mary felt a slight push on her back.

She tumbled forward, Mountie's hand slipping from her grasp. Mary landed hard on the ice-covered slide. It felt as if someone had punched her in the stomach. The ice was slick, and Mary could feel herself gaining speed. She grabbed for a bush as it whizzed past, but she couldn't hang on. Faster and faster she went, flying down the mountain, screaming hard, and her voice lost in the cold wind.

She reached out her hand again, hoping for something to slow her fall. Her palm smacked hard against something, and then she was flipping in an endless somersault, 'round and 'round. The school and the trees and the sky went topsy-turvy. Somewhere, up high, she could hear Lundy's dark, loud laughter.

Then she hit, plowing head first into the trunk of a big oak. The world was very quiet. Lundy's laughter had vanished. Mary's arm burned like fire. And though she'd stopped tumbling, her head was still spinning. She could hear the shouts of other children . . . then everything went black and silent.

Two

As Christy ran across the schoolyard with Mary in her arms, she said a silent prayer. *Please let Mary be all right. Please, God.*

Thank goodness Miss Alice was home today. Alice Henderson, who had helped found the school where Christy taught, lived in a small cabin near the main mission house.

"Miss Alice!" Christy called as she made her way up the cabin steps.

The door opened to reveal a lovely, regal-looking woman wearing a crisp blue dress. "Christy!" Miss Alice exclaimed. "What on earth—"

"She went down that icy slide the boys made," Christy said breathlessly.

Miss Alice held open the door, and Christy carried Mary into the cozy warmth of the cabin. Several of the local women were gathered by the fire, sipping tea from china cups.

"Prayer meeting," Miss Alice explained.

"That's my Mary!" cried a wiry little woman. Her thinning gray hair hung in a long braid down her back. She wore a drab brown skirt and a faded calico blouse buttoned high on her neck. Her milky blue eyes were set deep in skin criss-crossed with fine wrinkles. And her lips were stained by tobacco juice.

The woman bustled over, leaning on a wooden walking stick for support. "Put her down," she said to Christy. "She ain't your kin."

"I'm fine, Granny," Mary mumbled, still dazed by her tumble down the hill. She had blacked out for a moment after hitting the tree. But she'd regained consciousness by the time Christy reached her.

"Christy, this is Mary's great-grandmother," Miss Alice explained. "Granny O'Teale, this is Christy Huddleston, our new teacher at the mission school."

Granny did not answer. She tried to tug Mary out of Christy's arms, but Mary hung onto Christy's neck, refusing to go.

"Put her down, I'm a-tellin' you," Granny commanded. "Lordamercy, what have you done to my little Mary?"

"Some of the children said she was tripped," Christy said. "Is that what happened, Mary?"

The little girl nodded but refused to meet Christy's eyes.

"Who tripped you, sweetheart?" Miss Alice asked.

Mary buried her head on Christy's shoulder.

"Lundy Taylor," Christy muttered. "I've no doubt. He was up there with her."

"It might—" Mary began. "It might have been an acci-dent. I can't rightly recollect how it happened. We'uns was all up there, and it was mighty slippery-like."

Christy exchanged a glance with Miss Alice. Mary was

probably afraid to accuse Lundy. He terrified the younger children. Even Christy felt nervous around the hulking bully.

Miss Alice led Christy to her bedroom. Christy set the little girl down gently on Miss Alice's quilt-covered bed. Granny trailed behind, muttering something Christy couldn't quite make out.

"Why don't you two give me a minute to examine Mary and make sure she's all right?" Miss Alice said.

"I promise I'm fine, Miss Alice," Mary said quickly. "My arm's pretty banged up, is all."

"Looky here," Granny said. "Any doctorin' needs doin', I aim to do it."

"I'd be proud to have your help, Granny," Miss Alice said. "Why don't you let me take a look at Mary first? Then you can take over."

"I need to get back to the other children," Christy said. She hated to leave, but Mary did appear to be all right.

Mary's right arm was badly scraped. The beginnings of an ugly bruise were already visible. And there was a small knot where she'd bumped her head on the tree. But Mary was smiling calmly, apparently enjoying all the attention.

"I'll let you know how Mary's doing," Miss Alice said. "You go back to work."

Christy knelt beside the bed. "Mary, you take care of yourself, understand?"

Mary nodded. "Will you keep watch on Mountie for me? The others . . . They like to pick on her."

"Of course I will," Christy said. She took the little girl's tiny, cold hand in her own.

Suddenly another hand, withered and spotted with age,

grabbed hold of Christy's. "Don't you go near my girl, you hear?" Granny cried.

"But I was just—"

"You're nothin' but trouble, and that's for sure and certain," Granny said, releasing her grip. "We don't need no brought-on teachers comin' from clear across state lines to learn our children all kinds of citified notions. Flatlanders don't belong around here. Who asked you, anyways?"

"Granny," Miss Alice said firmly, "Christy is a wonderful teacher. She only meant to—"

"If'n she's so all-fired wonderful, how come my little Mary's lyin' here all black and blue?"

"It was an accident," Christy said. "It was recess, and I was watching the younger children playing in front of the school. I told them that only the biggest boys could slide down that hill—"

Granny pointed a long, yellowed fingernail at Christy. The old woman's eyes had a wild brightness in them. "An accident, heh? And how about Bob Allen? Were he an accident too?"

"Granny," Miss Alice soothed as she gently examined Mary's arm. "You know what happened. A tree fell on Bob Allen on his way to pick up Christy at the train station."

"And how come is that, I'm askin' you?"

"Probably because the branches were weighed down by snow. That was a very big storm we had, you remember."

Christy shuddered, remembering Mr. Allen's pale, nearly lifeless form. She'd felt so guilty, knowing he'd been hurt while trying to reach her. After Mr. Allen had been found, she'd helped the local doctor operate on him to relieve the bleeding inside his head. On her very first day in Cutter Gap, she'd ended up playing nurse in the most primitive conditions imaginable. It was truly a miracle that Mr. Allen had survived.

"Maybe it were the snow and maybe not." Granny narrowed her eyes. "Maybe this girl brought a heap o' trouble with her. Maybe she nearly killed Bob Allen with her comin', and now my little Mary."

"I'm right as rain, Granny, really I am," Mary protested. She cast Christy an apologetic look.

"Bob Allen is fine, Granny," Miss Alice said. "And Mary's going to be, too, from what I can tell."

"She's trouble, I'm tellin' you," Granny said, her voice trembling. She pushed her way past Christy. For a tiny old woman, she was surprisingly strong. "I can tell from a mile off when a person's cursed. And you, my girl, have the touch of it on you. The signs are all there."

"Cursed?" Christy repeated, half angry, half amazed.

"More'n likely ain't even your fault," Granny said. "Folks get cursed for all kinda reasons. Old Marthy coulda done it."

"You don't actually believe that, do you?" Christy asked.

"Seen it happen with my own eyes a hundred times. But mind you this, once you're cursed, you pass it on to everyone you're near. You best be headin' on back to where you came from before you do any more damage."

"Granny, I wish you'd give me a chance," Christy pleaded.

"Maybe you should be getting back to the other children," Miss Alice advised, sending Christy a look that clearly meant there was no point in arguing with Granny.

Christy sighed. "You take care, Mary," she said. As she turned to leave, she met Granny's eyes. "Nice meeting you,

Granny. Maybe sometime we can get together and talk some more."

The old woman glared back at her with such a frightful look that it was all Christy could do to keep from running from the cabin.

⌒⟶

Later that afternoon, Mary returned to class.

Christy was relieved to see that the little girl was all right, but the accident on the hill had left Christy feeling unsettled. First of all, she had to decide what to do about Lundy. No one would directly accuse him of anything, and Christy knew she couldn't punish the boy without proof. She finally decided that her only option was to keep a close watch on Lundy and his friends.

And then there was Granny O'Teale. Christy couldn't seem to forget the frightful look on the old woman's face. Of course, Christy didn't believe in curses. But it was hard to ignore the fact that, for whatever reason, Granny had decided Christy did not belong here in Cutter Gap.

She tried to shake off her nagging thoughts. She had other things to worry about this afternoon, like completing her first official week of school.

"As you are all aware," she said, leaning against her battered desk, "today marks the end of our first week of school." She was not surprised when a couple of the older boys—the troublemakers—began to whistle and clap.

"Thank you for that show of support, Smith and Wraight and Lundy," she said crisply. "Now, since it is Friday afternoon, I thought this might be a nice time, instead of working on our arithmetic, to hear from some of the older students.

You'll remember that on Wednesday I assigned a theme on 'What I Want to Do When I Grow Up.' Clara, why don't you start us off?"

Clara Spencer blushed, clearly flattered at the chance to go first. She was the daughter of Fairlight Spencer, a kind and gentle woman Christy had met on her journey through the mountains to Cutter Gap.

Clara straightened her patched cotton dress and cleared her throat. "When I grow up," she began, "I want to have lots of shoes—two, maybe three pairs, even. And I want a fine house with enough pans to cook in and a rug on the floor to sink my toes in." She looked over at Christy. "That's all, Teacher."

"Well, that was a fine job, Clara," Christy said. "An effort to be proud of." She pointed to Rob Allen, one of the older boys. "How about you—"

A deep snuffling noise, like a grunt coming from within the earth, cut her off in midsentence. Christy put her hands on her hips. "Wraight Holt, was that you?"

Wraight glared at Christy. "Weren't me. I ain't no pig."

"Now, that there's a lie if'n I ever heard one," said Smith O'Teale, Mary and Mountie's big brother. "I've done seen you at the supper table, Wraight Holt, and it ain't a pretty sight to behold!"

Laughter filled the room. "All right," Christy said. "That's enough." By now, she'd learned that she had to be firm, even when she wasn't feeling sure of herself. "As I was saying, why don't—"

Again, the grunting noise interrupted Christy. "What is that awful noise?" she demanded.

Creed Allen, a nine-year-old boy with tousled hair and

two missing front teeth, waved his hand frantically. "Teacher, I know what that there noise is. It's them hogs," he said. He tapped a bare foot on the wooden floor. "The ones underneath the school."

Christy sighed. In the Cove, as the area was often called, most hogs weren't penned. They wandered wherever they pleased, fattening themselves on beechnuts, acorns, and chestnuts. Some of them had even taken to sleeping under the schoolhouse, grunting with what had to be, Christy felt certain, the most repulsive sound in the world. It was hard enough teaching sixty-seven children without being interrupted by pigs.

"Are you sure it's the hogs?" Christy asked. "They aren't usually so . . . so vocal."

"Well, the thing of it is," Creed said, "it's a-goin' to storm."

"What does that have to do with the hogs?"

"They grunt extra loud afore the wind picks up," Creed explained.

"I'm sure that's just an old wives' tale, Creed."

"No'm," Clara broke in. "It's the truth, I promise you. They jerk their heads and grunt and carry on, sure as can be."

"I see," Christy said. These children were full of the strangest superstitions and mountain lore. She suspected that most of it was pure nonsense, but there was probably a grain of truth to some of the superstitions.

"Here, I'll show you," Creed volunteered, leaping out of his chair. He went to the center of the room where a trapdoor had been cut into the floor. A rope was attached to the door.

"Creed, I don't think—" Christy began, but Creed had already pulled the door open to reveal the crawl space beneath the school floor. There, grunting and grumbling, were several hogs.

"See?" Creed said. "See how they jerk their heads? Weather's changin' for sure."

Christy walked over to the edge of the trapdoor. "Yes, they certainly are noisy little fellows," she agreed. "Now, close that up, Creed."

"Want to pet one, ma'am?" Creed asked. "They're all whiskery and funny feeling."

Christy couldn't help making a face. "I'm not a big fan of hogs, to tell you the truth. Actually, I like dogs better."

"But hogs is the cleanest, smartest pets you ever did see, 'cept maybe for raccoons," Creed said.

"It's true," said Clara. "Our pet hog Belinda sleeps with me sometimes."

"Yes, I remember meeting Belinda when I visited your cabin, Clara," Christy said politely. "She was very, uh . . . very outgoing, for a hog."

"'Course she snores somethin' terrible," Clara admitted. "I drew a picture of her. Want to see?" Clara fumbled in her desk until she located a small piece of paper. Christy leaned down to examine the artwork. A carefully drawn hog grinned at her.

"Very nice, Clara," Christy said. "You'd almost think Belinda was smiling."

"Oh, but she is, Miz Christy! She smiles all the time, 'specially after supper. Pa says that's just her indigestion, like when babies get gas and they smile all funny-like." She lowered her voice. "Truth to tell, Belinda does get some mighty bad gas. 'Course, I love her anyway—"

Behind her, Christy heard giggling. She spun around.

Apparently, while she'd been talking to Clara, Creed had jumped through the trapdoor into the crawl space below the floor. The hogs looked quite happy to have some company.

"Creed, get out of there this minute!" Christy cried.

"I just figured you might want to meet one of the hogs," Creed said. He positioned a crate near the edge of the hole and herded one of the hogs toward it.

"Creed, I really don't need to meet any of the hogs," Christy said. "Now, come out of there, right now—"

But instead of Creed, a fat, grunting hog lumbered up onto the crate and out of the hole.

"I call that 'un George, on account of he looks like my Uncle George over in Cataleechie," Creed announced from the hole.

The hog sniffed the air curiously.

The children leapt from their seats and surrounded him, screeching with laughter.

"Go ahead and pet him, Miz Christy," Ruby Mae urged. "He's a nice enough hog, truly he is."

"I want that hog out of this classroom this instant," Christy said, but she couldn't help grinning as she said it. He looked so ridiculous, waddling around the classroom, snuffling and snorting like he owned the place. None of her teacher training had ever prepared her for this.

"Here's another one," Creed called. "I call this 'un Mabel, after my great-aunt, on account of he looks like my great-aunt Mabel over in Big Gap. 'Cept for the tail, of course."

Mabel eyed Christy doubtfully. She did not seem very happy to have joined the class. Clara reached out to pat the hog, and Mabel decided to run for cover. Unfortunately, she made a beeline for Christy. She didn't stop until she was hiding directly under Christy's long skirt.

"Help!" Christy cried. "Stop her!"

At the sound of Christy screaming, Mabel started to run again, pulling Christy's skirt—and Christy—along with her. Christy tumbled back onto the floor. Mabel peered out from under Christy's skirt and ran free, squealing in terror.

While Christy caught her breath, some of the children tried to round up Mabel. Unfortunately, Creed had released two more of the hogs in the meantime. Christy sat on the floor, watching with a mixture of amusement and horror as four hogs ran in crazy circles through the schoolroom. Students stood on tables and hid under desks, hoping to catch the animals. Screams and laughter filled the air.

Christy stood and brushed off her skirt. She had to get control of the situation, and fast.

First things first. She crossed the room and opened the door. "Mabel, George, and the rest of you hogs," she called, "school's over for you."

The hogs kept running wildly, ignoring Christy—and the door—entirely. They seemed to be in no hurry at all to leave.

"All right, now," Christy said with determination. "We've got to think like a team. I want all of you to get on the far side of the room. We're going to make a long line and herd these hogs right out of the door."

"Can't herd hogs, Miz Christy," Creed informed her as he finally climbed out of the trapdoor. "You can herd sheep and such. And cows, maybe. But hogs, they ain't much for bein' herded."

"Well, these hogs don't have a choice," Christy said.

She pushed some of the desks to the side of the room,

leaving the four hogs milling in the center. The children gathered in two long rows at the end of the room. Slowly they walked forward, arm in arm. Mabel ran straight into Clara Spencer's legs, then bounced off with an outraged squeal.

When the line of students was halfway across the room, George finally seemed to get the message. He scooted out the door with a last goodbye grunt. Soon two of his companions followed. Only Mabel remained. She didn't seem to want to go outside.

"Sorry, Mabel, you're being expelled," Christy said.

Mabel stopped. She stared at Christy and blinked. Then, with a defiant squeal, she made a mad dash for the coat rack. It toppled with a crash, landing right on top of the pig.

For a moment, silence fell.

"Oh, Mabel, are you hurt?" Christy cried.

The hog scrabbled beneath the pile of old coats and worn sweaters. Suddenly she emerged. A green, well-patched sweater draped over her shoulders, and somehow a battered felt hat had landed directly on her head. Garbed as such, she turned to look at Christy one last time, her snout high in the air, her hat at a jaunty angle. Then, with a queenly snort, she strode out into the yard.

Seconds later David Grantland, the mission's young minister, appeared in the doorway.

"Am I crazy," he said, scratching his head, "or did I just see a hog wearing a hat and coat come out of here?"

"Actually," Christy said with a smile, "It was a sweater."

"Ah," David said. "That explains everything."

Christy nudged Clara. "I know this sounds crazy," she said, "but I could have sworn Mabel was smiling when she left."

When they'd finally retrieved the sweater and hat Mabel had borrowed, Christy managed to get the class to settle down. She turned to Rob Allen. "Rob, why don't you read us your theme? And this time, if any hogs interrupt, just ignore them."

Rob headed to the front of the class. He was a tall, slender fourteen-year-old who had already proved to be a gifted student. "Sometimes," Rob read, "I get to feeling lonesome. I want to tell my thoughts, my good thoughts on the inside, to somebody without being laughed at. It would pleasure me to know the right way to put things like that on paper for other people too."

With a little nod at Christy, Rob returned to his seat. "Thank you, Rob," Christy said warmly. "I'm absolutely sure that someday you will make a fine writer."

The boy sent her a shy smile. Students like Rob gave Christy hope, but she knew it was just as important—maybe even more important—to encourage the difficult ones. Some, like Lundy, came to school with a chip on their shoulder and an angry word for anyone who got in their way. Others, like the strange, silent Mountie O'Teale, seemed completely unreachable.

Out in the yard, one of the hogs offered another ferocious grunt. The class erupted into laughter.

Christy turned to the window. Outside, the wind blew stronger. "It seems the hogs may be better predictors of the weather than I gave them credit for," she said with a laugh.

She noticed a group of women streaming out of Miss Alice's cabin. Apparently, the prayer meeting was breaking up.

Christy watched as Granny O'Teale, leaning on her wooden stick, slowly made her way toward the school.

Just then, the wind gave a sudden piercing howl, like a frightened animal. It was followed by a noise that sounded like rapid, muffled clapping.

The children fell silent. Christy gazed toward the ceiling. "Does anyone know where that sound is coming from?" she asked. Before anyone could respond, she had her answer. A sleek, black bird soared through the air above the children.

"A raven!" Mary cried.

The big bird swooped in a large circle, as if he were surveying the room. Several of the students ducked. A few covered their heads.

"Just what we need," Christy said as she sat down at her desk. "Another uninvited guest. How on earth did he get in here? And don't tell me Creed let him in through the trapdoor."

"Through the steeple up top, I'll wager," Creed said in a trembling voice. "It ain't all the way finished yet. I reckon that bird just sneaked his way on in."

"Nasty birds, ravens is," Ruby Mae said, eyeing the bird warily. "Like nothin' better than to pick out the eye of a lamb or a fawn."

The awful image made Christy shiver. "You mean when they find a dead one?" she asked.

"Naw. It's the eyes of livin' animals they like."

Christy watched the bird swoop and circle once again. It slowed as it neared her, then landed gracefully on her desk.

"Well," she tried to joke, "it's always nice to have another student. Mr. Raven, have you met Mabel and George? Perhaps our new arrival would like to share what he wants to be when he grows up."

A glance at the class told her they did not appreciate her joke. All eyes were locked on the shiny, strutting bird. Creed's hands were clenched in tight balls. Vella looked as if she were on the verge of tears. Ruby Mae was biting her lip nervously.

"Come on, now," Christy chided. "It's just a raven."

The bird cocked his head to one side, gazing at Christy with an eye like a black bead. She eased her chair back a few inches. She loved birds, but something about this one made her uneasy. He was too sure of himself, swaggering across her desk as if he were on some special mission.

Still, Christy was a "city gal," as the folks in Cutter Gap called her. It was understandable for her to feel a bit nervous. It seemed odd the raven was making these mountain children uncomfortable too. After all, they'd grown up surrounded by wildlife. They certainly hadn't been afraid of the hogs.

"Creed," Christy said, "open the door, would you? Maybe our uninvited guest will take the hint."

Creed ran to open the door. A blast of cold air filled the room.

"All right," Christy said to the bird, "it's been nice visiting with you, but it's time to go."

The raven did a little dance on Christy's desk, pecking at the surface and bobbing its head. Suddenly he stopped cold.

Christy heard a gasp. Granny O'Teale stood in the doorway, a horrified expression on her face. The old woman pointed a trembling finger at the raven.

"Mountie, Mary, Thomas!" Granny cried. "Get out here, now! I want all the O'Teale children to come with me."

The raven locked a glassy eye on Christy. It let out three

cries: *Caw! Caw! Caw!* Then, with a flourish of its wings, it whipped past Granny and sped out the door.

"Now, I tell you!" Granny yelled, beckoning with her arm. One by one, the O'Teale children began heading toward the door.

Christy stared past Granny at the darkening sky and dancing pines. "Why don't we call off school early today?" she said to the class. "I don't want you to get caught in bad weather, and I know that some of you have a long walk ahead. Class is dismissed. I hope to see many of you at church here Sunday morning. Assuming, that is, the weather doesn't cause us any trouble."

She was surprised to see the relief in her students' eyes.

Other days this week their departure had been filled with joyous laughter, dancing and running, and goodbye hugs. But today the students filed past Christy in a quiet, anxious procession. A few gave halting goodbyes. Creed and his friend, Zacharias Holt, paused just long enough to examine the top of Christy's desk, then dashed off through the door at high speed.

"Mary, I ain't a-goin' to tell you again," Granny cried, almost frantically.

"I'm comin', Granny," Mary called. "I'm just gettin' Mountie's coat on for her."

Christy watched as Mary and Mountie made their way through the maze of desks toward the door. As usual, Mountie's hair was snarled and her face smudged. She wore a dress two sizes too big for her, and over that a ragged coat with patched elbows and no buttons. She walked past Christy without expression. Her eyes were flat and dull. In her first week of teaching, Christy had never once seen Mountie smile or laugh.

"Mountie," Christy said gently.

The little girl paused. She did not turn.

"Mountie," Christy said again, touching the little girl's shoulder, "I just wanted to tell you how very lucky I feel to have you in my classroom. I hope we can be friends. I'd really like that."

Christy lifted her hand from Mountie's shoulder, and the girl moved on. Her face showed no sign she'd understood Christy's words. How could a little girl so young and innocent seem so dead inside?

"Take care of that arm, Mary," Christy called as the two girls joined Granny.

Granny shook a finger at Christy. "Stay away from my girls, you hear? I'm a-warnin' you. I seen all I need to see. You're bad luck, you are."

With that, Granny yanked the two girls away. Christy watched Mountie's small bare feet padding across the snow. Big, feathery flakes were starting to fall.

"What is that old woman so afraid of?" Christy whispered. "I just want to help."

As if in answer, one of the hogs under the school let out a very uncivilized grunt.

"Another vote of support," Christy said. She smiled, but as she watched Mountie clasp Mary's hand and slowly disappear into the dark woods, her grin vanished.

High up in a swaying pine, the shiny black raven stared down at Christy with a haunting glare.

Three

"AND THAT'S THE END OF IT," GRANNY SAID FIRMLY AS SHE led Mary and Mountie into the O'Teales' tiny cabin.

The girls' mother, Swannie O'Teale, was poking at the fire. "End of what?" she asked. She held out her arms, and Mary and Mountie ran over to give her a hug.

Granny dropped into her rocker as the door swung open and Smith, Orter Ball, George, and Thomas dashed inside. Smith was carrying a snowball.

"Out with that," Swannie O'Teale said wearily as she sat.

Six-year-old Thomas ran to Granny's side. "Did ya tell Ma?" he asked excitedly.

"Tell me what?" Mrs. O'Teale asked.

"About the raven," Thomas said.

Smith tossed the snowball out the door. "Today a raven, big as you've ever seen, came a-flyin' straight into the school," Smith said, his voice low and spooky.

"Big as an eagle, it was," Orter Ball added.

George nodded. "Swooped around that room and went straight for that teacher like a huntin' dog sniffin' out a coon."

Mrs. O'Teale pulled Mountie into her lap. "Ravens is evil birds. Where'd it come from, do you 'spect?"

"Came out of nowheres," Smith said. He made a low moaning noise, like the wind outside. "Just like a witch-bird."

"Stop it, Smith, you're a-scarin' me," George whined.

"I 'spect it came in through the steeple up top," Mary said. "The preacher ain't finished it all up yet. I'll bet there's holes up there. Raven probably came in to get warm." She smiled at Granny. "Or like Teacher said, maybe he wanted some book learnin.'"

Granny shook a finger at her. "This ain't nothin' for you to go makin' light of, girl. A raven's a bad omen. Outside a house is bad enough, but inside, like this 'un . . ." She shook her head. The fire reflected in her eyes. "This flatlander's bringin' a heap of badness with her, I'll wager."

"Tell me the rest," Mrs. O'Teale urged. "What happened to the raven?"

"He done flew straight to that teacher's desk like he knowed right where he was a-goin," Smith said. "And then he locked a beady eye on her and let out three loud calls for all the world to hear."

"*Caw! Caw! Caw!*" Orter Ball and George piped up.

"And then Creed Allen opened up the door, and that bird flew out like he'd done what he set out to do," Smith finished.

A hush fell over the cabin. Outside, a branch cracked and tumbled, bouncing off the roof. The wind moaned and whistled. Mountie reached for Mary's hand and squeezed it.

"That mission school is the work of the devil!" Granny hissed. Her eyes were wide and filled with fear.

"Might be you're right, Granny," Mrs. O'Teale said, nodding.

"I told you no good would come of sending the children to those people. They ain't like us. And now you have the proof of it, plain as day. Tell her about your arm, Mary."

"Ain't nothin', Mama," Mary said quickly, but it was too late. Her mother had already noticed the ugly mark.

"Mary! Did that teacher—"

"No, Mama, no! Lundy Taylor done tripped me, is all. I fell down the slidin' hill and hit a tree."

"It's another sign," Granny said, her voice quavering. "That, and the tree a-fallin' on Bob Allen, and probably this storm to boot."

"Granny, it's January," Mary argued. "We have storms like this all the—"

"Don't go sassin' me," Granny said. "That raven went straight for that city gal. And that's a sign she's cursed, sure as I'm a-sittin' here."

"I say she's a witch," Smith said.

"Smith don't like her 'cuz she told him not to talk out of turn," Mary said. "Teacher's not bad, Mama, I promise you. She's got this way of talkin', so pretty it well-nigh sounds like music. And a red sweater so soft you'd a-swear it were made of sunrise clouds. And her eyes! There be something magic about them—"

"Black magic," Granny cried. "Already she's got you under her spell, girl." Granny got up from her rocker and went to Swannie O'Teale's side. "You mustn't send these children back to that mission school," Granny said. "No good will come of it. Wherever that teacher gal goes, troubles will follow like the moon follows the sun. I'm a-warnin' you."

"But we wanted the children to have some book learnin',"

Mrs. O'Teale said slowly. "I was hopin' they could learn Latin, all proper-like."

"Look what happened to Bob and to Mary," Granny argued. "Could be worse, much worse, next time."

"I s'pose yer right."

"But Mama—" Mary cried. Her heart sank. She could already tell that her mother was going to give in to Granny's demand.

"No point argufyin' with Granny," said Mrs. O'Teale. She hesitated. "'Course, I would like to get to church on Sundays still. Do you think that would be safe, Granny? After all, she were at church last Sunday and nothin' bad happened."

Granny stroked her chin. "Coulda been lucky that time. I'd advise against goin' back."

"On the Lord's day," Mrs. O'Teale said, "with the whole of the Cove there to ward off her curse? And no teachin' a-goin' on, just proper preachin'?"

"Well, I s'pose that might be safe," Granny gave in reluctantly. "If'n I brew us up some powerful herbs to ward off that gal's curse, we might just could go. I'd have to think on it a spell. A little garlic, a pinch o' dill to ward off the evil. A clover leaf, if'n I can find some dried . . . If I put together a proper recipe, I 'spect we could go to church."

"Too bad for that," muttered Smith.

"Mind you, now," Granny warned, "you can't be a-lettin' her in on why you're wearin' my recipe. Gal with a curse on her that strong, she'll be able to work against all my medicine. So you'uns keep your mouth hushed when you're over to the church."

"So we don't have to go to that mission school no more?" Smith asked.

"Looks like not," said Mrs. O'Teale.

"Good thing," Smith said. "She was way too bossy for a gal woman, if'n you ask me."

"Please, Mama—" Mary began.

"Hush now," Granny interrupted. "I need to figure on what herbs and such will ward off a curse that strong."

"Could you make it somethin' that don't smell too bad, Granny?" Orter Ball asked. "'Member that time we was afraid of catchin' sick and you done made us rub that lard mess on ourselves? Stank to high heaven, it did."

"You stop your fussin' and be thankful you got a granny who knows such things," Granny replied. She cast a warning look at Mary. "And not another word about that teacher gal, you hear?"

⌐#⌐

Mary lay in her bed that night, listening to the wind howl and carry on. Creed Allen had been right when he'd told Teacher it was going to storm. Tree limbs heavy with snow cracked like lightning. The icy wind found every chance it could to sneak through holes and cracks. Mary shivered beneath her thin blanket.

Mountie lay beside her on a straw mattress on the floor. Three of their older brothers slept in the loft—a hole cut in the ceiling that led to a small space they reached by ladder. Their mama and papa slept in the far corner of the room. Thomas, the youngest, slept near them. Their oldest brother, Wilmer, who had fits, slept in a sort of half bed, half pen, in the corner. Granny, on account of her age, had the only bed off the floor, and it was just a straw mattress on some crates to keep her away from the cold floor.

It was not much of a cabin, Mary knew. Most of her friends at school had nicer ones. Cleaner, anyway. Once, when she'd gone to the Spencers' cabin to play with Zady, she'd seen a bunch of flowers in a bowl, just sitting right there on the eating table for no reason except to look pretty. Miz Spencer was like that, always laughing and singing and picking flowers.

Mary's mother never sang. She had saggy shoulders, as if she were carrying some awful load of rocks she could never put down. Sometimes Mary wondered why that was. It could be that Wilmer, who'd been simple minded ever since he was born, made their mother extra tired. He was a heap of trouble and pain, drooling and muttering and running away when no one was looking.

Even though Wilmer barely knew who Mary was, she loved him just like she loved all her brothers. She even loved Smith, although he had a bit of a mean streak running through him. But Mary saved most of her love for Mountie, because her sister seemed to need it more than any of the others. Their mama and papa were too busy to pay much attention to the silent little girl, and Mary had always been the one to watch out for her. Granny loved Mountie as much as Mary did, but she had a hard time showing it.

Mary rubbed the bruise on her arm. Already it was the color of a ripe blueberry. Granny had said it was Teacher's fault, but Mary didn't see how that could be. Lundy Taylor was always causing trouble. They couldn't expect Teacher to fix the whole world on her first week, now, could they?

But she hadn't said that to Granny. She loved her great-grandmother, but she was afraid of her too. Granny had a hot temper, and a way of looking at the world that other folks didn't have. Some even said she had second sight and could see clear into the future. And it was true enough that Granny could see signs and portents where no one else could.

The wind let loose a powerful shriek. In the corner near the fire, Granny snored away. Mary thought again of the strange raven who had flown to Teacher's desk that afternoon. Remembering the bird's evil black eyes, she shuddered.

She nudged Mountie, who rolled over and smiled. "Mountie," Mary whispered, "do ya s'pose that raven comin' to Teacher's desk meant anything bad? Bad the way Granny says, I mean?"

Mountie gazed at Mary thoughtfully. She hardly ever spoke. Once or twice Mary had heard her say a clear word, but mostly Mountie just communicated in grunts and nods. Still, Mary knew her sister understood everything. She could see it in Mountie's eyes.

"Some folks say ravens near a house is a bad omen," Mary continued. "So what do you s'pose a raven comin' right into school like that could mean? What if Granny's right and it's a powerful bad sign?"

A head dropped down from the ceiling. It was Smith. "Can't you quit your jabberin'?" he demanded loudly. "Good thing cat's got Mountie's tongue for good, or I'd have to listen to two gal folk carryin' on like a couple of crows. You ask me, that teacher's trouble, and Granny's right about her."

"You just don't like her 'cause she makes you and Lundy Taylor mind," Mary said.

"You think that raven was some kind of accident?" Smith said.

"Could be."

"Naw. It was a sign for sure."

"Smith?" Mary whispered. "S'pose I wore Granny's herbs and kept a-goin' to school? You think Granny'd let me?"

"Ask her, why don't you?" Smith wadded up a piece of straw and tossed it at Granny's bed. The old woman stirred slightly, grunting. "Granny!" Smith said in a loud whisper.

"No, Smith!" Mary hissed. "Don't go wakin' her. You know how ornery she gets."

Granny's eyes fluttered open. "What in tarnation is your trouble, boy? Can't you see I'm a-tryin' to sleep? Not that it's easy, mind you, with that storm wallopin' the walls."

"Go ahead," Smith urged Mary. "Ask Granny."

Orter Ball and George stuck down their heads. "*Caw! Caw! Caw!*" they cried in unison.

"Next bird I hear, I'm a-shootin' for," warned Mr. O'Teale.

Granny yawned. "Ask me what, child?"

"S'posin' I wore your herb recipe and kept on a-goin' to school?" Mary asked softly. "Me and Mountie, we could sit way in the back, where nothin' bad could get to us—"

"A curse like that don't care what row you're a-sittin' in, girl," Granny said.

Mary gazed at her great-grandmother. In the firelit room, her eyes blazed with life. It was almost as if she were enjoying what was happening to Teacher, the way some people like to watch a storm unwind.

"'Night, Granny," Mary said. With a sigh, she leaned back. "I guess that's all the book learnin' for you and me for a while, Mountie," she whispered.

Mountie didn't react. But much later, when everyone else was asleep, Mary wasn't surprised when, over the moaning of the endless wind, she heard her sister softly crying.

Four

"I JUST DON'T UNDERSTAND IT," CHRISTY SAID AT DINNER Saturday night.

"Give them time, Christy," Miss Alice advised as she reached for a biscuit. "Rule number one here in the Cove: everything takes time."

"Sometimes centuries," joked David.

All the workers at the mission gathered in the main house for dinner each evening. Although Christy had only been there a few days, she was already beginning to feel at home. Miss Alice, of course, made that easy. So did David, who had only been there a short time himself. David's sister, Ida, was more difficult—a crotchety, no-nonsense sort. And then there was Ruby Mae, who was staying at the mission temporarily because she was not getting along with her family. Ruby Mae seemed to have appointed herself as Christy's official shadow. She followed Christy everywhere.

"But why would Granny O'Teale react that way to me?" Christy asked for what seemed like the millionth time. "I understand that she was upset about her great-granddaughter.

And maybe she was right. I do need to find a better way to keep an eye on the children at all times."

"Sixty-seven children, Christy," David said. "Nobody can keep track of all of them every minute. Trust me, I know." He helped out with Bible and arithmetic classes in the afternoon.

"I wouldn't worry too much about Granny, Christy. Her reaction isn't unusual," Miss Alice said. "These mountain people are proud of their heritage, and stubborn too. It's going to take them a while, maybe even a long while, to accept you. It's taken me years to be accepted."

"But she sounded so . . . so angry," Christy said. "As if she blamed me for Bob Allen's accident. She said she saw signs that I was cursed."

Ruby Mae dropped her fork. "Granny knows all about signs and such," she said nervously.

"Come on, Ruby Mae," David scoffed.

"No, I swear, it's true," Ruby Mae cried, pushing her long red hair out of her eyes.

"Give me one example," David challenged.

"How about the time Granny O'Teale was charming a wart off her finger, when along comes Mr. McHone. He laughs at her, and Granny warns him, says, 'You'll be sorry for laughin'.' And sure enough, the next day Mr. McHone's got a hundred warts growing on his finger in the exact same spot." Ruby Mae shook her head. "She's powerful, Granny is. And smart to boot."

"Powerful silly, is more like it," David said. "I—"

He was interrupted by a loud knock at the front door. Miss Ida went to answer it.

"Doctor MacNeill," she said, "come on in out of that cold. Would you like a bite to eat?"

The doctor—a big, handsome man with unkempt red hair and deep lines around his eyes—came inside. "Thanks, Miss Ida," he said, "but I've eaten already. I'm on my way home and just thought I'd do myself a favor and thaw out a bit, if you don't mind." He took off his gloves. "Strangest weather I've seen in a long while. Snow yesterday, hail today—" His eyes fell on Christy. "Well, if it isn't Florence Nightingale," he said, breaking into a broad grin. "Did Miss Huddleston tell you how she helped with Bob Allen's surgery?" he asked the rest of the group. "She turned the nicest shade of green you've ever seen." He winked at Christy.

She felt a blush rise in her cheeks.

The doctor placed a hand on her shoulder. "Actually, she was a godsend," he said. "Don't know what I would have done without her."

"Granny O'Teale seems to think I'm the cause of Bob's accident," she said.

The doctor laughed as he pulled up a chair near Christy. "Don't take it to heart."

"That's what everyone keeps telling me," Christy muttered.

"So how goes the first official week as teacher?" the doctor asked.

Christy shrugged. "It's hard for me to say. There are so many children, and we need so many supplies . . . I guess I'll find a way to handle it all."

"She's doing great," David said. "We're very proud of her."

Miss Ida cleared her throat loudly. "Well, I think I'll be getting these dirty dishes to the kitchen."

"Let me help, Miss Ida," Christy said, pushing back her chair.

"Oh, no, that's not necessary," Miss Ida said. She cast a

glance from the doctor to her brother. "You've obviously got your hands full. Ruby Mae can help."

Ruby Mae grabbed a dish and followed Miss Ida. "Do you think Miz Christy's got two suitors already?" she asked loudly as they left the room.

Christy covered her eyes. She needed to have a talk with Ruby Mae about learning to whisper. "Ruby Mae's very, uh . . . imaginative," she said.

"Quite a talker, that one," Miss Alice agreed, smiling at Christy's discomfort.

"Doctor MacNeill, I was wondering about something—someone, actually," Christy said, anxious to change the subject. "Is there anything that can be done for Mountie O'Teale? She barely speaks, and when she does, it's so garbled she sounds like a frightened animal. It breaks my heart."

The doctor shook his head. "Swannie tells me she's been like that for years."

"Swannie?"

"Mountie's mother," he explained. "My guess is it's more emotional than physical, but I can't even be sure of that. As far as I know, Mountie won't communicate with anyone."

"She's been that way as long as I've been at the mission," Miss Alice said.

Ruby Mae returned for more dishes. "Maybe she's got a spell on her," she suggested.

"Ruby Mae!" Christy exclaimed.

"It happens!" Ruby Mae insisted. "I heard tell of a boy over in Cataleechie. He had a spell on him so's all he could do was mew like a kitten. Lasted two whole months. Even when that spell was took off him, he never did drink milk normal after that. Always had to lap it out of a bowl."

Christy smiled sadly. "I almost wish that there was such a thing as spells and that that was the cause of Mountie's problem, Ruby Mae," she said. "Then we could just look for a way to break the spell."

<hr />

After the doctor, David, and Miss Alice had left for the evening, Christy went up to her room. Miss Alice had her own cabin, and David lived in a nearby bunkhouse. That left Christy, Miss Ida, and Ruby Mae in the main house, a white three-story frame building with a screened porch on each side. Compared to Christy's home back in Asheville, North Carolina, it was very plain. It had no telephone, no electricity, and only the barest of furnishings. She often missed the polished mahogany dining room table back home, the thick Oriental rugs, the lace curtains, not to mention the indoor plumbing.

Still, she was growing accustomed to her simple room at the mission. It was a stark contrast to the frills and pastels of her old bedroom—just a washstand with a white china pitcher and bowl, an old bed and a dresser with a cracked mirror, a couple of straight chairs, and two cotton rag rugs on the cold bare floor.

But this room offered something her old room could not: a view so breathtaking that each time she looked out her window at the haze-covered peaks of the Great Smoky Mountains, she felt a little closer to God. Mountain ranges folded one into the other, touching the clouds, a sight so peaceful and calming that already she had begun to think of it as *her* view, a source of hope and strength. Even tonight, with the wind whipping fiercely and the moon and stars hidden, she could see those peaks in her imagination with perfect clarity.

Christy reached into the top drawer of her dresser. Underneath a neatly folded white blouse lay her black leather-covered diary. She had brought it with her from Asheville, promising herself she would write down everything that happened to her at the mission—the good and the bad. This was, after all, the greatest adventure of her life, and she wanted to record every moment of it.

She'd had to argue long and hard to convince her parents that a nineteen-year-old girl should venture off to a remote mountain cove to teach. She had first heard about the mission and its desperate need for teachers at a church retreat last summer. Somehow she had known in her heart that she was supposed to go teach in this mountain mission school. There was so much less here materially, but in many ways life in Cutter Gap was much richer than her old life in North Carolina, filled as it was with tea parties and dress fittings and picnics.

Christy climbed onto her bed. Propping the diary on her knees, she uncapped her pen and tapped it thoughtfully against her chin. Where to begin? It had been two days since she'd written.

Saturday, January 20, 1912
   My first week of school completed! Hooray!
   I have put up with freezing temperatures, vicious bullies, and raccoons in desks, and still I've survived to tell the tale. Perhaps I will make a good teacher yet.
   David and Miss Alice are encouraging but realistic. "You cannot change the world overnight," Miss Alice keeps saying.

I can't admit this yet—not to them, not to anyone . . .
It's even hard for me to write this down in my own private
diary. But the truth is I feel like such an outsider here.
David seems to feel like an outsider too. Even Miss Alice
says it took her years to be accepted by the mountain
people. But the littlest things make me feel I'll never really
belong here.

I came to school my first day in my fancy leather shoes,
only to see practically all the children barefoot in the
January snow. When I talk, they still giggle and whisper.
(David says this is because my "city accent" is as strange
to their ears as their way of talking is to me.) And when
someone like Ruby Mae Morrison (my very own personal
shadow, it seems) talks constantly about the strangest
things, I sometimes wonder if we aren't from different
worlds.

Ruby Mae's nonstop chattering has me seriously
considering making cotton plugs for my ears. Miss Alice
has a Quaker saying she often uses: "Such-and-such a
person is meant to be my bundle." Well, like it or not, Ruby
Mae is clearly going to be my *bundle.*

Sometimes, I think I am beginning to make progress.
Yesterday, Mary O'Teale and Ruby Mae and some others
were telling each other "haunt tales" about an old witch,
and when I tried to reassure them not to be frightened of
the dark, I think I actually managed to reach them. Of
course, that was easy for me to understand—I had the
same fears as a child. (When I remember the ghost stories
George and I used to tell each other, I still get the shivers!)

But later, when Lundy Taylor (another big
problem) tripped little Mary and sent her falling down
the icy mountain slide the boys had made, Mary's

great-grandmother blamed me. It wasn't just that Mary had been hurt. It was something more—some deep fear and resentment for anyone not from the Cove. Try as I might, I'm certain that in a million years Granny O'Teale will never like me.

Time. Maybe that's all it will take. I'll make friends with these people. I'll come to understand them. And maybe as I do, I'll come to understand my purpose in the world.

A loud knock at her door interrupted Christy. She slipped the diary under her pillow and capped her pen. "Yes?"

"It's me, Ruby Mae."

Christy sighed. "Just a second, Ruby Mae."

When Christy opened the door, Ruby Mae burst into the room as if it were her own. "I was thinkin' you might like some company."

"Actually, I was about to get ready for bed."

Ruby Mae examined her reflection in Christy's cracked mirror. "I think the preacher and the doctor, they both got a hankerin' for you, Miz Christy."

Christy laughed. "Ruby Mae Morrison," she said, "what am I going to do with you?"

"You never know," Ruby Mae said with a grin. She ran a hand through her snarled, shoulder-length red hair. Halfway down, she winced.

"How long has it been since you combed your hair, Ruby Mae?" Christy asked. "Or shouldn't I ask?"

"Factually, I lost my comb. Disremember when. Onliest comb ever I had too."

"There are some bad tangles," Christy said. "Come, sit

here on my bed." She retrieved her own comb from her dresser.

Ruby Mae plopped down on the bed. "I'll try not to holler when you hit them mouse nests," she vowed.

Christy started, gently pulling the comb down.

"Ohoo-weeee!" Ruby Mae cried.

"Sorry."

"Don't matter. What do you aim to do when you get it all combed out?"

"How about nice long braids? Like Miss Alice's?"

"Be tickled to death with braids. But you'll have to learn me how."

"Braiding's easy. I'll teach you."

Braiding hair is not the only thing I'll have to teach Ruby Mae, Christy thought as she tried to unravel the snarls. Ruby Mae's sole idea of cleanliness was to wash her face and hands a few times a week—never a full bath. It was not pleasant to be near her. And it wasn't just Ruby Mae; it was all the children. After the hair combing, maybe Christy would suggest a bath to Ruby Mae in the portable tin tub and then make her a gift of a can of scented talcum powder.

"I'm going to have to yank a little, Ruby Mae," Christy said when she reached a particularly stubborn snarl. She pulled as gently as she could, but Ruby Mae leapt back against Christy's pillow, howling.

"I'm really sorry, Ruby Mae," Christy apologized.

"What's this?" Ruby Mae asked, pulling at the corner of the diary Christy had pushed beneath her pillow.

"Oh, that? Nothing. It's private," Christy said quickly.

Ruby Mae frowned. "I just mean," Christy continued, "it's a place where I write down things."

"What sorts o' things?"

"Feelings, dreams, hopes. What happened today. People I meet, places I go. Diary things."

"Am I in there?"

Christy smiled. "The special thing about a diary is that it's private."

"What's 'private'?"

"Secret. Things you keep to yourself."

Even as she tried to explain, Christy recalled her visit to the Spencers' cabin—seven people living in two tiny rooms and a sleeping loft. How could she expect these children to understand privacy? It was a luxury they couldn't afford.

Christy divided Ruby Mae's hair into strands and began to braid. When she was done, Ruby Mae gazed at her reflection in amazement.

"Lordamercy, Miz Christy, you done worked a miracle!" Ruby Mae cried. "I look as purty as a picture, if I do say so myself."

Christy smiled. "You do indeed." She watched as Ruby scampered off, talcum powder in hand, on her way to take a full bath. Once the lively girl had gone, she closed the door and pulled out her diary.

A small victory, just now with Ruby Mae. No more snarls!

Is this why I came all this way? To braid a tangle of red hair? To pass out scented powder?

Maybe so. Miss Alice says that if we let God, He can use even our annoyances (take Ruby Mae, for example) to bring us unexpected blessings.

Today braids. Tomorrow the world!

Five

On Sunday morning the driving snow had turned to driving rain. Clouds hung low, sifting and churning like a dark sea. Thunder rattled the windowpanes.

As Christy, Miss Ida, and Ruby Mae crossed the yard to the church, Miss Ida tried to share her umbrella. But as they made their way across the plank walk David had installed, everyone was splattered by the icy rain. The combination of snow and rain had turned the yard into a sea of mud.

"If it's this hard for us to get here," Christy said as they crossed, "I wonder how everyone else will make it."

"Oh, they'll make it," Miss Ida assured her. "Don't forget that church is the great social event here in the Cove. Remember how full the pews were last week?"

When Christy entered the room that had served as her school all week, she was surprised to see that it was nearly as full as it had been last Sunday. She settled into the pew nearest the pulpit. As she watched children enter with their families, she waved and smiled whenever she recognized a familiar face. Oddly, only a few of them waved back, although she caught plenty of stolen glances in her direction, not to mention whispers and pointing. She was surprised when she called out hello to Creed Allen, only to be greeted by a stiff half smile and an uncomfortable nod.

Christy was relieved when she felt a friendly tap on her shoulder. "Howdy, Miz Christy," Fairlight Spencer said.

Christy smiled at the woman who'd befriended her on her journey to the mission. From the beginning, Christy had sensed that she and Fairlight could someday be good friends. Seeing the woman's warm smile today made Christy certain of it.

"Fairlight," Christy exclaimed. "It's good to see a friendly face."

"Oh, they'll warm up to you. Just give 'em time. My children can't stop talkin' about school. It's 'Miz Christy this' and 'Miz Christy that.' John tells me you might be a-findin' him a new arithmetic book."

"He's got a real head for math," Christy said. "John's going to be a joy to teach." She held up a finger. "And speaking of teaching, I promised you we'd get together for some reading lessons."

"Oh, but you're just gettin' settled in," Fairlight protested.

"Tell you what. Give me a couple more weeks to get settled, and then we'll get started."

"I'd be mighty pleased," Fairlight said. She nodded toward the back pew. "I gotta get myself a seat before the preacher starts."

Christy watched Fairlight settle behind her with her husband, Jeb. As Christy waved to Jeb, she again noticed the whispers and stares her presence seemed to be causing.

"Am I crazy?" she whispered to Ruby Mae. "I feel like everyone is staring at me."

"No'm." Ruby Mae glanced over her shoulder. "They's starin', all right. I reckon it's 'cause you're new and all."

"But they weren't acting like this last week," Christy said.

"It is strange," Miss Ida said. "They're usually a more rambunctious crowd than this." She wiped a drop of rain from her forehead. "Perhaps it's this odd weather."

"Well, once the service gets going, they'll probably relax," Christy said uneasily.

"The way they carry on during David's services is undignified, if you ask me," Miss Ida said, shaking her head. "Singing and clapping and bouncing. David does the best he can."

Christy smiled. It was true that the services here in Cutter Gap were nothing like what she was used to at her church back home.

Before long, the first hymn was in full swing, and the atmosphere in the church did seem to change. The people sang joyously, tapping their toes and clapping their hands. No one seemed to be staring at Christy any longer.

Thunder rumbled like a bass drum as they launched into a second hymn:

> *It's the old ship of Zion, as she comes,*
> *It's the old ship of Zion, the old ship of Zion,*
> *It's the old ship of Zion, as she comes.*
> *She'll be loaded with bright angels, when she comes,*
> *She'll be loaded with bright angels . . .*

Suddenly Christy felt an uneasy sensation. She turned her head slightly and instantly realized why.

Three pews back sat Granny O'Teale. She was not singing.

Her milky eyes were riveted on Christy. She was wearing an old black shawl, and around her neck sat a crude necklace tied with a string. Mountie sat beside her.

Christy tried to send a smile to the girl. Granny wrapped an arm around Mountie protectively.

Christy turned around, but as the hymn continued, she imagined Granny's gaze sizzling across the crowded room like lightning. Christy had seen something in those tired old eyes. If she didn't know better, she would have called it fear.

When at last it came time for David's sermon, Christy began to relax. It was silly to worry so much. Of course these people were staring at her. She was from someplace far away, and she was bringing new ideas to their children. Their curiosity was only natural. Perhaps they'd reacted to her this way last week and she had just been too preoccupied to notice.

David was dressed in fine style, even though his congregation wore plain work clothes. He had on striped pants, a white shirt, and a dark tie. His black hair was carefully combed. He spoke in a deep, rich voice, measured and dignified.

"I plan to preach to you today on Mark 6, verses 30 through 46, the story of the Feeding of the Five Thousand. Although I must say that with this weather, maybe I ought to be talking about Noah and his ark." The room filled with laughter.

"But before I begin, I want to introduce a welcomed addition to Cutter Gap: our new teacher at the mission school, Miss Christy Huddleston."

Christy felt a blush creep up her neck. David hadn't done this last week. Perhaps he'd understood how nervous she'd been about meeting so many new people. But making a point of introducing her today, with everyone acting so strangely, did not seem like a good idea, either—at least as far as Christy was concerned.

"Christy, why don't you stand and let the folks get a look at you?"

Christy sent David a pleading look, but he just grinned back mischievously. Reluctantly she stood, turning toward the suddenly hushed group.

"Look, Mama, it's Teacher!" Vella Holt cried out, waving.

Christy gave a nervous smile, then quickly dropped back down to the bench.

"I'm sure you'll all do your best to make Miss Huddleston feel welcome. She's a wonderful teacher and is going to be a real help to this cove—"

Just then someone let out a scornful laugh.

Christy had an uneasy feeling as she recognized the source. She turned around to see Granny smirking back defiantly.

Miss Ida laid a comforting hand on Christy's. "Don't pay them any mind," she whispered. "They just don't know any better."

Christy looked at the woman next to her in surprise. It was the first time Miss Ida had revealed such kindness. But before Christy could thank her, Miss Ida withdrew her hand and returned her attention to David.

"I'm certain," David continued, his voice taking on a sterner note, "that you will all give Miss Huddleston a chance to prove what a wonderful teacher she is."

Jagged lightning lit up the sky, followed by an ear-splitting clap of thunder. Christy shifted uncomfortably in her seat. It was going to be a very, very long service.

"You can say I'm crazy all you want," Christy said to David as they finished up their pancakes at breakfast the next morning, "but I'm certain there was a lot of whispering and staring going on at church."

"Well—" David sipped at his cup of coffee— "perhaps they were just entranced by your charms."

"Stop teasing," Christy said. "I'm serious, David. And you heard that snort of disapproval. It was Granny O'Teale, I've no doubt of it."

"Could have been one of the hogs," David pointed out. "Talk about your hog heaven. With all that mud, they were having a real party out there."

Christy laughed. "Well, I've got more important things to worry about today, like figuring out how to get more organized with the children's lessons. To begin with, I thought about dividing them into grades, instead of this boys-on-one-side-of-the-room, girls-on-the-other nonsense."

Ruby Mae looked up in alarm. "No'm, I can't sit by no boy!" she cried. "That ain't no courtin' school!"

"Of course it isn't," Christy said reasonably. "But it just makes sense to seat children of the same level together, whether they're boys or girls."

"Makes no sense a-tall!" Ruby Mae exclaimed.

David cast Christy a smile. "Seems you do have other things to worry about today," he said.

Miss Alice gazed out the window at the unceasing, icy rain. "Have you ever seen it rain so hard?" she asked. "I'll be surprised if all your students make it today, Christy."

"That might be just as well," Christy said, grinning. "I was feeling a little outnumbered last week!"

With a last sip of coffee, Christy gathered up her notebook and sweater and headed across the plank walk to the schoolhouse. Ruby Mae followed behind, carrying Miss Ida's umbrella. David had already lit a fire in the schoolroom stove, and the chill was gone from at least part of the room. Christy and Ruby Mae straightened school desks while they waited for the children to arrive.

By seven fifty, Christy was beginning to worry. Only about a third of her sixty-seven pupils had shown up. "Where is everybody?" she asked Creed Allen. "Do you think the weather's keeping them away?"

"Yes'm," Creed said in an unusually soft, polite voice. "Could be the weather. Strangest thing I ever did see, snowing somethin' fierce, then rainin' like it ain't never goin to stop." He cocked an eye at Christy. "You ever seen such weather, Teacher?"

As Christy opened her mouth to answer, she noticed that all of her students were watching her expectantly. A strange quiet had fallen on the room. "Well, Creed," she said, "come to think of it, I can't say that I have." She leaned against her desk, smiling at her pupils. "I must say, this is the most well-behaved I've seen you since we started school. Is it just because there are fewer of you? Or is it the weather?" She paused. "Come on, somebody tell me. To what do I owe this wonderful behavior?"

Nobody answered. Creed studied his dirty thumbnail. Vella Holt twirled one of her pigtails nervously. Even Lundy Taylor, sitting sullenly in the back of the room, seemed subdued.

"Well," Christy said, "I guess I should just enjoy my good fortune." She reached for her attendance book. "Let's see. Who is missing today? I don't see any of the O'Teales or the McHones."

As Christy took the roll, she strolled up and down the rows of students, noting each empty desk. With every step, she sensed eyes following her, just the way she had in church. *This is odd*, she thought. The children hadn't acted this way last week. They'd been barely able to control their excitement. Why would they be treating her differently now?

Stranger still was the odd aroma, bitter and pungent, that seemed to follow her as she walked. Smells were nothing new, of course. These were children who had never been exposed to the basics of hygiene. Already Christy had come to hate her too sensitive nose. She had found some relief by carrying a handkerchief heavily soaked with perfume up her sleeve.

But this smell was something altogether different. It reminded her of the horrid-smelling medicine her mother had made her take as a child when she'd had the flu. It smelled of strange, bitter herbs and even a touch of garlic.

She considered asking someone about the smell, then hesitated. After all, maybe one of the children had been given some kind of homemade medicine. She didn't want to embarrass anyone by drawing attention to the odor. Still, it was odd that no matter where she went in the room, the scent seemed to follow her.

The sky was darkening with each passing moment. Christy lit two kerosene lamps. As she set one on her desk, she said, "How about a song to chase away the gloom?" She knew the children loved to sing. Although they didn't know some standards like "America," they knew all kinds of ballads from their Scots-Irish and German heritages. "How about 'Sourwood Mountain'?"

A few children nodded.

"When I asked you if you wanted to sing that last week, you were all practically jumping out of your seats!" Christy exclaimed. "What is wrong with—"

A deep growl of thunder interrupted her.

"Now, don't tell me a little thunder's bothering you," she chided. She touched Vella's shoulder and the little girl jumped. "I'm sorry, Vella, did I scare you?"

"No'm, I ain't scared," Vella said quickly. "I ain't scared of you 'cause I got my—"

"Hush up, big mouth." Her sister, Becky, yanked on one of Vella's pigtails.

"What were you going to say, Vella?" Christy asked, kneeling down to the little girl's side.

"Nothin'. I ain't scared, that's all."

Christy frowned. She eyed Becky, but the older girl just stared straight ahead. Her hands were clasped together as if she was praying.

"All right, then," Christy said. "'Sourwood Mountain.' I'll start it up, but you know the words much better than I."

She went to the front of the room. The kerosene flame flickered, sending long shadows dancing up the walls.

"'I've got a gal in the Sourwood Mountain,'" Christy sang. To her surprise, only a few half-hearted voices joined in.

Christy sighed, hands on her hips. "Is this the same class that was here last week?" she teased. "If I didn't know better, I'd say someone had put a spell on you."

Several of the students gasped. Creed's eyes went 'round.

"Ain't no spell, Teacher," he blurted. "I promise we is us, just like always. Ain't no spell or nothin'!"

"All right, Creed, relax. It was just a joke—"

Just then, lightning as bright as the noon sun sent a blinding flash through the room. Christy heard something cracking, a sound like the slow splitting of wood. Rain pelted against the windows. Deafening thunder, like nothing she had ever heard, shook the sky, drowning out the cracking sound.

And then it happened. Christy heard it before she saw it—the eerie, musical sound of glass shattering as a tree limb lurched through one of the windows, reaching into the schoolroom like a huge hand.

Desks overturned as children screamed and ran, and rain fell in torrents. Everywhere she looked, Christy saw mud and dirt and branches and glass and splinters of wood.

"It's just a branch," Christy called to the terrified children cowering near the door. "Lightning hit that old pine, is all. Is anyone cut? Anyone hurt at all?"

Some of the children were sobbing. A few hid behind desks. Christy ran from child to child, checking for glass cuts or scrapes.

"Vella, are you all right?" she demanded.

The little girl could only manage a terrified sob.

"Creed?" Christy called.

"Yes'm," he answered in a squeak of a voice. "I ain't hurt none."

Christy climbed over the great wooden carcass in the middle of the room. The smell of pine needles and mud had replaced the strange odor that had filled the room only moments before.

"Well, it looks to me like we may just have to move school

over to the mission house for the rest of the day," Christy said as she checked Ruby Mae for cuts. No one responded. The children just kept staring at Christy, dazed and sobbing, as if they were afraid to take their eyes off her for even a moment.

At last Christy felt certain that no one had been hurt. She was grateful to see that the children had been spared injury. But no matter how hard she tried, no matter what words she used, she could see the dark fear in their eyes as she tried to comfort them, and something told her it was not the storm that they feared.

Six

"THAT LIGHTNING WAS A SIGN, I'M A-TELLIN' YOU, SWANNIE," Granny said Friday morning as she settled into her rocking chair on the O'Teales' front porch. "It's a good thing we ain't lettin' the young'uns near that city gal." She reached out her hand and pulled Mountie into her lap, rocking quietly as she stroked the girl's hair.

Mary stood in the yard, listening to her great-grandmother talk. She tossed corn kernels to the chickens, who strutted about the yard as if they owned it. Ever since Granny had heard about the lightning strike at the mission school on Monday, she hadn't stopped talking about it.

It hadn't taken her long to hear, either. News had a way of traveling fast in Cutter Gap. Of course, by now almost everybody had heard about the raven's visit to the mission school at the end of last week. They'd also heard about Granny's carefully prepared mixture of herbs and roots. "Smells plumb fearsome," Creed Allen had whispered to Mary when his mother had stopped by the O'Teale cabin to get some of Granny's "curse chaser," as Granny called it. She placed a spoonful of the smelly mixture on a little piece of rag, then tied it up with a string. It was to be worn around the neck under the clothes—at all times, if it could be tolerated.

Mary thought Creed was right—the mixture did smell horrible—but Granny knew her potions well. And for whatever reason, nobody who'd been around Miz Christy had been hurt yet. Fact was the tree hit by lightning hadn't done much damage other than scaring some of the children. That very afternoon the preacher had boarded up the broken window.

Mary tossed the last of the corn to Lucybelle, her favorite chicken. She gazed toward the path that led to the school and let out a long sigh.

"Look at that face," Granny chided. "You look like you lost your last friend."

"Granny," Mary asked slowly, choosing her words with care, "if'n the raven and the lightning were signs that Miz Christy's cursed, how's come none of us were hurt at church last Sunday or the Sunday afore that? She was right there in a pew a-sittin'?"

"It's the Lord's house on Sunday, child."

"But the children who keep a-goin' to school, they're still all right. Creed said so on Wednesday."

Granny considered. "Well, most all of 'em is wearin' your granny's secret curse chaser, for one thing. And for another, that don't mean bad things can't still happen. Those parents is takin' an awful risk, if'n you ask me."

"Creed said his mama figures he'll be safe if'n he wears your recipe. She wants real bad for him to learn Latin, 'cause that's a proper education. So she's lettin' him and the other children keep a-goin' to school."

Granny held out her hand. Mary squeezed it gently.

"You don't need no schoolin' anyway, Mary," Granny said. "You're already smart as a whip."

Mary thought of Teacher's magic blue eyes as she'd read them the Twentieth Psalm the first day of school. Her voice had been magic too. She'd promised them she would teach them how to read words out of real books and how to write the way she did on the blackboard, with letters full of loops and curves. She'd talked of faraway places they would learn about, places with funny names that twisted on the tongue.

And she'd told them wonderful stories that came straight out of her own head—made up, but real as could be. Sometimes Mary told Mountie stories like that, late at night when they were too cold or too hungry to get to sleep. What a gift it would be to write them down all nice and proper on a chalkboard, or maybe even on a piece of paper Mary could keep forever and ever.

Mary pulled on her herb necklace. "Granny," she asked, "can I take this off'n me sometimes? It stinks somethin' terrible, and it itches me too."

"That's its power," Granny said firmly. "You leave that right around your pretty neck."

"But Teacher's nowhere near here."

"You leave it on, just in case. She weren't too near Bob Allen when that tree nearly killed him, now was she? A bad curse can travel a long ways."

"What would happen if Teacher found out I was wearin' this thing?"

"She ain't a-goin' to find out because you ain't a-goin' anywheres near that school." Granny gave a playful tug on Mary's hair. She'd been in a fine mood the last couple of days, Mary had noticed. "And ain't you just as glad? Didn't you miss your ol' Granny, sittin' in that school all day long?"

"Sure I missed you, Granny." Mary hesitated. "But just for the sake of askin', what would happen if she done found out?"

"Then the curse would take over," Granny explained. "It's the secret of the recipe that gives it all its power." She winked. "How about a smile for your poor ol' granny, now?"

Mary did her best. "I gotta go get some more kindling," she said. "Fire's gettin' low."

"Ain't no need to fuss." Granny wriggled her bare feet. "Gonna be a warm 'un for Jan'ry, now that the rain's done stopped."

Mary's mother peered out the cabin door. "Strangest weather I ever did see."

"It's the brought-on teacher," Granny said.

As she headed for the edge of the woods, Mary considered her granny's words. Here in the mountains, strange weather was hardly unusual. And lightning strikes—well, they were as common as ticks on a hound. The McHones' cabin had nearly burned down last summer after being struck by lightning.

She bent down to pick up a stick. Everything was far too wet to make good kindling. There was no point in looking. Granny was right, anyway. It was going to be a warm one today.

Granny was right a lot, she thought. She'd known Miz Spencer's last baby was going to be a boy. Of course, that could have just been good guessing. She knew that corn should go in the ground when the dogwood whitens, but then a lot of folks knew that. She said you should never step to the ground with one shoe on and one shoe off, because for each step, you'd pay with a day of bad luck. But that was just common sense.

Granny had also told Mary not to climb to the top of the hickory tree near Blossom Ridge or she'd fall and break into a thousand pieces, but she had anyway, and she'd had a fine view of the sun coming up, all rosy and full of itself. She'd told Mary not to bother telling Mountie stories, because Mountie couldn't understand them, but Mary told them anyway. And she knew from the way Mountie smiled at her that she always understood every word.

It wasn't that Granny didn't love Mountie, of course. You could see she did, from the way she rocked Mountie to sleep at night. It was just that sometimes even Granny was wrong.

It was a hard thing to be thinking. It made Mary feel mixed up inside. She didn't like that feeling, not at all.

"Mama?" Mary called. "I'm a-goin' down to the Spencers' to see Zady."

"Take Mountie," her mother called back. "Mary? You hear me?"

But Mary was already winding her way through the trees. She headed, fast as her feet could carry her, down a path that didn't go anywhere near the Spencers' cabin.

It went straight to the mission school.

⌐#⌐

"Twelve, thirteen, fourteen." Christy sighed. Fourteen students today. At this rate she'd be down to zero soon.

"Has anyone talked to the O'Teale children?" she asked. "Or the McHones or the Holcombes?" Even Lundy Taylor and Wraight Holt were gone today. As strange as it seemed, she was sorry to lose them. "With the weather better today, I'd hoped to see more of you."

Christy's gaze fell on Creed. The little boy's neck was flushed, and his eyes were oddly bright.

"Creed, are you feeling all right?"

"Yes'm," he said in the same flat voice he'd been using all week. "Just a little scratchy on my chest and neck is all."

"You might be coming down with something," Christy said. She reached over to feel his forehead. The boy flinched at her touch.

"You do feel a little warm. Are you sure you feel all right?"

"Yes'm."

"What's that string around your neck?"

"Just a—for decoration, Teacher."

Christy shook her head. She'd noticed that several of the other children were wearing pieces of string or yarn around their necks. There seemed to be something attached to the strings, but since the children wore the necklaces under their clothing, she couldn't tell for sure. Whatever the odd necklaces were, Christy had begun to suspect that they were the source of the bitter medicinal smell wafting through the room. By now she'd almost grown used to the odor.

Even Ruby Mae had taken to wearing one of the necklaces. Yesterday at dinner, it had been hard to ignore.

"What is that awful odor?" Miss Ida had demanded.

"I don't smell nothin'," Ruby Mae had said quickly.

"You'd have to be missing your nose not to smell it," David had said.

But Ruby Mae had just smiled innocently. When she'd left the table, David had whispered, "Probably just some mountain remedy. A lot of the children seem to be wearing those obnoxious things around their necks. Just think of it as another teaching challenge!"

Christy had laughed, but today, breathing in the horrible smell, she wondered how much longer she could stand it. Of course, at the rate her class was disappearing, she wouldn't have to tolerate the smell much longer.

The door opened, and Christy turned to see Mary O'Teale standing breathlessly in the doorway. Mary stared at all the empty seats, then smiled shyly at Christy.

"Mary!" Christy cried. "What a nice surprise! We've missed you. Come on in. As you can see, there's plenty of room."

"I missed you, too, Teacher," Mary said, touching her neck self-consciously. She hesitated, then sat down on the girls' side of the room next to Ruby Mae.

"Were you unable to come because of the weather?" Christy asked hopefully.

"Weather. Yes'm," Mary said. Her cheeks were flushed and damp. "For certain that was part of it."

"And will Mountie and your brothers be coming today?"

Mary shifted uneasily in her seat, scratching hard at her upper chest. "I can't rightly say."

"Mary," Christy said. "Are you all right? You look like you might be getting some kind of rash."

"Just some itchin' that needs scratchin' is all," Mary assured her.

Christy wondered again if the children were coming down with something. She knew that because the mountain people shared their drinking water and lacked the most basic hygiene, disease often spread like wildfire through the Cove. Typhoid, a particularly deadly disease, had hit the area many times. Christy wondered if she should have Doctor MacNeill take a look at the children. She'd seen him over at the mission house earlier today, talking to Miss Alice.

"It could be you're coming down with something contagious, Mary," Christy said.

"I reckon I don't know what you mean by 'contagious,'" Mary admitted.

"That means a sickness that other people can catch," Christy explained. "Creed looks a little under the weather—and so do some of the others, come to think of it. Do you mind if I check your neck, Mary?"

Mary clutched at the string around her neck. "Oh, no, Teacher," she cried. "I be fine, really I am."

Christy bent down. She could see a horrible, bumpy red rash making its way up the little girl's neck. "Mary," she said softly, "what is that necklace you're wearing? I notice a lot of the children have them."

"Ain't nothin' special," Mary said, looking away.

Christy sighed. She was getting nowhere fast. Her class smelled like a medicine factory. Several of her students were growing peculiar rashes. Most of them were wearing strange necklaces they refused to discuss. And many had simply stopped coming to school at all.

Christy had talked to Miss Alice and David about the diminishing student population. They were as mystified as she was, but both had reassured Christy that it was only a matter of time before the mountain people began to accept her. She just wasn't sure she could wait that long.

"I am going to ask you this just once," Christy said, in her no-nonsense teacher tone. "Someone has to tell me the truth. John? Creed? Mary? Ruby Mae?"

Ruby Mae leaned over and whispered something to Mary.

Mary whispered back. Both girls locked their eyes on Christy.

"Ruby Mae?

"Yes'm?"

"Is there anything you want to tell me?"

Ruby Mae twisted a strand of red hair around her finger. "No, Miz Christy, I reckon there ain't nothin' I want to tell you."

"But you're usually such a chatterbox."

"Yes'm, it's true. My mouth don't open just for feedin' baby birds," Ruby Mae agreed. "And I don't mean to be ornery, but I reckon there's not a solitary thing I want to be tellin' you right now."

"Fine," Christy said, struggling to rein in her anger. "At the noon recess, I'm going to have Doctor MacNeill and Miss Alice take a look at those odd rashes." She opened her tattered history book. "In the meantime, why don't I read you the story about George Washington and the cherry tree? Do you all know who George Washington was?"

Creed raised his hand.

"Yes, Creed?"

"I reckon he was pa of the whole U-nited States."

"Father of our country. Very good, Creed. And one of the things he's most famous for is saying he could not tell a lie."

She studied the anxious faces of her audience. "Perhaps that's a lesson you could all learn from."

⟞⟝

"I'm a-tellin you, these rashes is part o' the curse," Creed whispered in hushed tones behind the school during the noon recess. "I thought I'd be safe comin', what with Granny O'Teale's herbs and such." He kicked at a pebble with his bare foot. "Truth is I kinda like comin' to school. And Teacher seems so all-fired nice and everything, even if'n she is a flat-lander and talks right peculiar. But now—" he scratched frantically at his upper chest— "now I ain't so sure I'm ever comin' back. I itch somethin' fierce."

Ruby Mae leaned against the building, careful to avoid a brown tobacco stain. "I don't know what to think anymore. These rashes is plumb unnatural. Factually speakin', it makes me mighty nervous to be sharin' the same roof with someone who might just have a curse a-hangin' over her."

"Could be Teacher's found out about Granny's magic recipe," Creed suggested, eyes wide with fear. "Do you s'pose she's fightin' back with spells of her own?"

"Swear to Josh-way," Mary said, "I've had rashes like this before from Granny's potions. One time—" she lowered her voice— "she got to fussin' 'cause Smith saw a pure black skunk. Not a stripe on that animal anywheres. Granny said it was an omen. Said we was all a-goin' to come down with the typhoid. So she made up this mixture, with lard and bear grease and who knows what all else in it. Smelled to high heaven, it did. She made us smear it all over ourselves for three days solid. Thought I'd like to die from the stink of it."

"So what happened?" Ruby Mae asked.

"Well, we'uns broke out with boils all over. You talk about itchin'? I tell you, I cried somethin' awful, it itched so bad. Worse than this, even," Mary said, pointing to her chest. "'Course," she added, to be fair, "we never did come down with the typhoid, so maybe there was somethin' to Granny's potion, after all." She sighed. "I feel all switched up inside, like there's two whole Marys in there, argufyin' over whether to trust Teacher or not."

"I might just have a way to figure out the truth of things," Ruby Mae said. "You two can come if'n you want, but you gotta be quiet as mice."

"Will it tell us if'n Granny's wrong?" Mary asked.

"Could be. We're a-goin' to sneak into Miz Christy's room and find out the truth."

Mary nodded. "Let's do it, quick-like," she said. "I have to know if I'm right about Teacher, one way or the other."

Seven

"MISS IDA, HAVE YOU SEEN MISS ALICE?" CHRISTY ASKED as she stepped inside the mission house.

Miss Ida looked up from the pie crust she was rolling out in careful, even strokes.

"I thought you were upstairs," she said, her brow knitted. "Didn't I just hear you—" She shrugged. "I must be imagining things. Miss Alice is in her cabin, I believe. She's meeting with Doctor MacNeill."

"Doctor MacNeill's still here?" Christy said. "That's wonderful. I need to have him look over some of the children." She hesitated. "Actually, I was wondering if I could recruit you for a minute or two . . ."

"Me?" Miss Ida demanded. "I don't know the first thing about teaching."

"I just need you to keep an eye on things while I go get Miss Alice and the doctor," Christy explained. "There aren't that many children to watch, actually."

Miss Ida sighed. "I'm right in the middle of an apple pie."

"How about this?" Christy said. "I'll do all the cleaning up around here for the next couple of days, if you can just spare me ten minutes."

"No need," Miss Ida said, wiping her hands on her apron. "My work is never done around here, anyway. What would you all do without me, I wonder?"

"So do I," Christy said with a grateful smile.

As she headed across the main room toward the front door, Christy thought she heard whispering from the stairwell. She paused, listening. Nothing. But as soon as she started walking again, she was almost certain she heard a muffled giggle coming from the second story.

Christy crept up the stairs, careful to avoid the one near the top that squeaked. Her bedroom door was half closed. She could hear the shuffle of feet, then whispering.

"Ruby Mae?" Christy asked, pushing the door open.

Someone screeched. Christy entered the room to see Ruby Mae standing near the bed, hands clasped behind her back. Mary O'Teale and Creed Allen were sitting at the foot of the bed.

"What on earth are you three doing in here?" Christy cried.

"We . . . uh, we was just a-lookin' for . . ." Mary's voice trailed off.

"For somethin'," Creed volunteered.

"That much is obvious," Christy said. She took a step forward and Ruby Mae instantly took a step back, tumbling onto the bed. "What's that behind your back, Ruby Mae?" Christy asked.

"Behind my back?" Ruby Mae repeated in a shrill voice not at all like her own. "Behind my back? Well, like as not, I 'spect that would be my fanny." She offered Christy a weak smile.

"Very funny, Ruby Mae." Christy put her hands on her hips. "You three do understand that this is my room, and that you do not just go poking around other people's property without their permission?"

All three slowly nodded.

Christy reached for Ruby Mae's arm. "Come on, Ruby Mae," she said gently, "hand it over."

"No!" Creed cried suddenly, leaping off the bed. "Don't hurt her, Teacher!"

"Creed, of course I wouldn't—"

Ruby Mae's face was white as she reached out a trembling hand. She was holding a black leather book.

"My diary?" Christy gasped. "You were reading my diary?"

"We was just tryin' to find out if you—" Ruby Mae seemed to lose her voice.

"If I what?" Christy pressed.

Ruby Mae looked at Creed. Creed looked at Mary. Their faces were pale, their foreheads beaded with sweat.

Christy approached Mary. The little girl was trembling, but when Christy knelt beside her, Mary managed a small smile.

"If I what, Mary?" Christy asked in a whisper. She held out her hand and Mary reached for it. Her fingers were like tiny icicles.

"You know, Mary," Christy said, "I miss seeing Mountie. I miss all the children, of course, but I've especially missed seeing you two. When you came back today, I was so happy that I said a little prayer of thanks. Do you think Mountie misses me?"

Mary gave a tiny nod.

"And have you missed me too?"

The girl answered with another nod.

"Whatever you tell me, Mary, you can trust me. I won't let any harm come to you. I'm your friend. I came here to help you. Do you believe me?"

Mary thought for a minute, working her small mouth. At last, she nodded again.

"Then you can tell me, Mary. What are you afraid of?"

"Don't, Mary!" Creed cried. "If'n you tell her, then the secret recipe won't work no more."

Mary bit her lip. She looked into Christy's eyes as if she thought she could find something she needed there. "Granny . . ."

"Yes?"

"Granny says . . ." Mary cleared her throat.

"Granny says what?" Christy encouraged.

"She says you're cursed," Mary blurted. "She says you brought bad things to Cutter Gap and that we'uns shouldn't go to school no more!"

Christy blinked. So that was it. That explained the missing children. That explained the look of fear on the faces of the few students who still dared to come to school.

She pulled Mary close and gave her a hug. The bitter smell of herbs made her eyes burn. Gently, Christy pulled on the yarn necklace around Mary's neck. At the bottom was a small piece of old cloth, filled with what felt like dried bits of plants.

"Did Granny make this necklace for you?" Christy asked.

"Yes'm."

"Why?"

"It's a curse chaser. To ward off your bad spell and keep us safe."

Christy frowned at the awful rash on the little girl's neck. "Well, I'm not so sure she's accomplishing that." She looked over at Creed. "Are you wearing one too?"

Creed nodded. "Most all of us are, Teacher. Ma said the only way she'd let me go to school was if'n I wore this and kept my distance. 'Course some parents just flat-out said no." He cocked his head at her, a confused look on his face. "What's wrong?"

"Well, I figured you'd be sore as a skinned owl when Mary done told you. You ain't a-goin' to put a spell on us, is you?"

"Creed, of course not. That's nonsense." Christy could barely control the anger in her voice. "I don't understand how you children could believe such a silly notion—" She stopped herself. It wasn't the children who deserved her anger. It was Granny O'Teale and the other adults who'd allowed such superstitious foolishness to fill the heads of these poor children.

"Thank you, Mary," Christy said gently, "for telling the truth."

"You won't tell on me to Granny, will you?" Mary asked in a quavering voice. "I weren't even supposed to be here."

"Of course not." Christy smiled. "Creed and Mary, I want you to come with me. Doctor MacNeill needs to take a look at those rashes."

As Christy started for the door, Ruby Mae rushed past, nearly knocking her aside.

"What's wrong, Ruby Mae?" Christy asked. "It's going to be all right. I'm not mad."

Ruby Mae paused in the doorway, glaring.

"Come on," Christy said. "You've hardly spoken a word."

"Reckon I ain't got nothin' to say," Ruby Mae muttered. "Reckon that's the way you like it, anyways."

With that, she turned on her heel and ran down the stairs.

<hr />

"You won't believe what I'm about to tell you!" Christy cried as soon as Miss Alice opened the door to her cabin. Christy stomped inside, motioning for Creed and Mary to follow.

"Relax, Christy," Miss Alice urged. "I can see you're very upset."

"It's just that—well, do you have any idea what people in the Cove are saying about me?"

Doctor MacNeill was sitting in a rocker. "Hmm, let me see. That you're the finest teacher they've ever seen in these parts?"

Christy paced back and forth on the polished wooden floor, practically choking on her anger. "They—"

"Let me try again," the doctor interrupted with a grim smile. "They're saying you're cursed and that the only way to go near you is with a handful of foul-smelling herbs?"

Christy stopped midstride. "You're telling me you knew?"

"Relax, Miss Huddleston," he said. He paused to take a long puff on his pipe. "I only just heard myself." He nodded to Miss Alice.

"I stopped by the McHones yesterday evening to check on that broken arm of Isaak's," Miss Alice explained. "That's when I first got wind of Granny O'Teale's theory about you."

"Theory!" Christy practically spat out the word. "Look at that rash on Mary, Doctor. Creed has one too. I think it's from Granny's herb concoction. I'll bet half the population of the Cove is breaking out!"

The doctor called Creed over and examined the little boy's rash. "How long have you had this, Creed?"

"I disremember exactly. Last couple days for sure."

"How about you, Mary?" Miss Alice asked gently.

"It don't bother me none, Miss Alice," Mary said. She took a nervous step back. "You ain't a-goin' to tell Granny I told on her, are you?"

"Are you afraid she'll hurt you, Mary?" Christy asked.

"No'm. Mostly I'm afraid she'd be a-thinkin' I didn't believe."

"Believe?" Christy echoed.

"In her powers. Her second sight and such."

"Your secret is safe with us, Mary," the doctor assured the little girl.

"Why don't you two run on out to the schoolyard?" Miss Alice suggested. "The doctor and I will be by with some medicine to make that itching stop."

As soon as Miss Alice opened the door, Creed ran outside. But Mary paused in the doorway.

"Teacher?" she said softly.

"Yes, Mary?"

"I'm purty sure that Mountie misses you too. She can't exactly say it just so, but I can tell."

Christy nodded. "Thank you, Mary."

Miss Alice closed the door, and Christy sank into a chair. "Where on earth did that old woman come up with such a notion?" she demanded.

"Superstitions grow like weeds around these parts," the doctor said. Carefully he placed some fresh tobacco in the bowl of his pipe. "You've still got a lot to learn about the mountain people. Granny is known in the Cove as a fine herbalist. Some of her knowledge is sound enough, and some of it is nonsense. But her word is still gospel."

"But what made her turn on me? Why me?"

Miss Alice touched Christy's shoulder. "There's no use looking for a logical reason, Christy. Perhaps it was Bob's accident, or Mary's fall. Perhaps Granny just feels threatened by all the changes going on here in the Cove."

Christy jumped from her chair. "I need to reason with her. Maybe I can explain to her why she has nothing to fear from me."

The doctor laughed. "No use trying to use logic with someone like Granny. You can't fight mountain superstition. Remember right before Bob Allen's operation? His wife ran into the cabin where we were operating and swung an ax into the floor. Then she tied a string around Bob's wrist."

Christy nodded. She remembered all too well.

"Well, I could have argued with his wife till spring, telling her that a string won't keep disease away, and an ax won't keep a person from hemorrhaging. But meantime, Bob would have died." He shook his pipe at Christy. "And if you try to argue these people out of their superstitions about you, your dreams for the school will die too."

"But if I don't fight back somehow, there won't be a school," Christy cried. "I've lost most of my students already, Doctor. Pretty soon I'll be teaching a roomful of empty desks."

Miss Alice added a log to the fire. "Christy," she said, rising, "our job here at the mission is to demonstrate that there's a better way than fear and superstition. We want to create an atmosphere where hearts can be changed. If we preach to the hearts of men and women, the fruits will follow. But it's no good tying apples onto a tree. Soon they'll be rotting apples."

Christy clenched her fists angrily. "But that could take forever, Miss Alice. The doctor's been here for years, and the mountain people still don't understand even the most basic principles of hygiene."

The doctor stiffened. "And you, Miss Huddleston, have been here two weeks, and you think you can change the world?" He gave a dark laugh. "I wish you luck."

"Time," Miss Alice said, "is a great healer, Christy. Give Granny and the others time. They will come to trust you."

Christy took a deep breath. Maybe Miss Alice and the doctor were right. Or maybe they were just tired of fighting back. And in any case, they weren't "cursed." She was.

"Miss Alice," Christy said firmly, "I understand what you're saying, but I have to try to save my reputation. I'm going to the O'Teales'. I'll ask David to watch the class for the rest of the day."

"Miss Huddleston, I wouldn't—" the doctor began, but Christy shot him a determined look, and he held up his hands.

"Will you give me directions to the O'Teales' cabin?" Christy asked. "If not, I'll ask Mary to tell me the way."

"Of course I will," said Miss Alice. "I'd advise against this, but if you insist on going, I want you to remember one thing: for all her ignorance and superstitions, there's a good heart inside Granny O'Teale. There's a good heart inside all God's children. Look hard enough and you will find it."

"I've just one question," said Doctor MacNeill. "What are you going to say when you get there?"

Christy headed for the door. "Good question, Doctor. Guess I'll figure that out on the way."

Eight

As Christy trudged along the muddy path, she took in deep lungsful of the mountain air, trying to let go of her anger. Again and again, Mary's fearful face came back to her. She thought of the way Creed had cringed at her touch, the way Vella had jumped when Christy touched her shoulder, and the way Ruby Mae had glared at her so coldly.

Granny had done this. Granny O'Teale had, in the space of a few short days, managed to undo Christy's first halting attempts at befriending these children. And how? By playing on their fears and superstitions and ignorance.

Suddenly, just ahead of her down the path, Christy saw some dark blobs scattered over the snow for several yards. As she got closer, she realized the blobs were bloodstains and bits of torn fur—some black, some reddish brown. She gasped. Some poor little rabbit had been caught by another animal and torn to bits.

Quickly Christy carved a wide path around the dead animal's remains. She wished her mind were a blackboard so she could wipe away what she had just seen. Why did nature have to be so vicious?

Why, she wondered, *do people have to be so vicious?*

The O'Teales' tobacco barn was just up ahead, so she knew their cabin wasn't far. Soon it came into view beyond a stand of pines. In the yard, the trampled-down, muddy snow was littered with rags and papers and junk. Pigs and chickens wandered at will. A big black pot was turned on its side, rusting. No effort had been made to stack the firewood; the logs lay in disarray where they had been tossed.

Christy paused at the edge of the yard. Suddenly she realized the debris was even worse than it had looked from a distance. The yard was covered with filth—both human and animal filth. The chickens were pecking at it. The pigs were rolling in it and grunting. Christy lifted her skirts, picking her way across the yard. Wasn't there an outhouse in the backyard? Weren't they teaching the children anything?

Swannie O'Teale appeared on the crude porch. She was a tall, slender woman with stringy, dirty-looking blond hair. Her eyes looked dull and tired and sad. But there was something else there too. Fear—that was it. It was the same look Christy had seen in her students' eyes.

"Mrs. O'Teale," Christy called. "I'm Christy Huddleston, the new teacher."

"I know who you are," Swannie O'Teale hissed. "And if'n you know what's good for you, you'll get. Granny's out gatherin' bark for her potions, and if'n she sees you—"

"I don't want to hurt you, Mrs. O'Teale. I want to help. You've got to trust me."

"Can't trust the likes of you. You be cursed. Granny said so," Mrs. O'Teale said, backing into the open doorway. "Get now." She clutched the yarn necklace around her neck. "Get now, I'm a-tellin' you!"

Christy took another step. Even from several feet away, the stench coming from the cabin was horrible. A low half growl, half screech met her ears. In the dim light beyond the door, she could make out a boy in his teens wearing a tattered sweater. Saliva drooled from the corners of his mouth and trickled through the grime on his chin.

"Ah . . . hello," Christy said.

"That be Wilmer, my firstborn."

Christy remembered hearing that one of the O'Teale children had epileptic seizures, or "fits," as the mountain people called them.

The boy pointed to a tin plate of cornbread on a nearby table. "Unh-um-humh. Ah-hmm."

"Hungry, Wilmer?" Mrs. O'Teale said wearily. "Don't go squawking."

What must it be like, to have to care for Wilmer and the other children in these awful surroundings? Christy wondered. *Such poverty. Such misery.* Staring into Mrs. O'Teale's weary, fearful eyes, Christy felt her anger drain away.

"Mrs. O'Teale," Christy said. "Where are the other children?"

"Out with Granny, 'cept for Smith. He's helpin' his daddy. And Mary, she done run off over to the Spencers this mornin'. That girl can be a heap of trouble—" She caught herself. "I can't be a-talkin' to the likes of you."

"Mary's a sweet girl," Christy offered. "And the boys—"

Mrs. O'Teale scoffed. "Smith! You're plumb crazy if'n you think he's a sweet 'un!"

"Well, he does get a little rambunctious," Christy conceded.

She had the feeling that if she just kept talking about the children, she might get somewhere with Mrs. O'Teale. Despite her warnings to Christy, the woman seemed anxious to talk. "But I think rowdier when he and Lundy Taylor get together. They sort of provoke each other."

"Those boys stick together like sap and bark," Mrs. O'Teale said. "I don't know how you manage with all those young'uns in one place."

"It must be hard for you too," Christy said, glancing over Mrs. O'Teale's shoulder at Wilmer.

"Naw," Mrs. O'Teale said. She seemed to be losing her fear. "Not too bad. I got Granny here to help me."

"And does she help?"

"Lordamercy, yes! Loves these children more'n I do, I sometimes think. She's especially partial to the girls." She winked. "Though she won't let 'em know it, mind you. Don't want 'em gettin' all high and mighty with the boys. But many's the night I seen her watchin' Mary and Mountie when they're a-dreamin'—" She paused, straightening her faded calico skirt. "I—I shouldn't be lettin' my mouth run on like this." She lowered her voice. "I know you mean well, Miz Huddleston, and maybe you ain't cursed and maybe you is. But it'd be best if you get goin' right quick."

She couldn't go, not now. Christy could sense that she was making progress. If she could just win over Mrs. O'Teale, maybe Granny would follow.

"Mrs. O'Teale, do you think I could step inside for just a moment to sit? I'm not used to walking such long distances, and I could use a rest before I head back to the mission."

"I just don't rightly think—"

"A minute, that's all," Christy said, practically pushing her way inside.

"You're buyin' yourself one passel o' trouble," Mrs. O'Teale said, still holding her necklace. She watched warily as Christy sat down on one of the two chairs in the room. "Granny'll give you more trouble than ever you saw in all your born days."

"See?" Christy smiled, trying hard not to stare at the horrible filth or breathe in the stench. "Nothing's happened. No one's hurt. Mrs. O'Teale, there's been a terrible misunderstanding. I didn't come here to hurt your children. I want to help. I know what Granny's said about me being cursed, but that's not true."

A loud noise filled the room. Christy jumped. Wilmer had dropped his tin plate. He pointed to it and laughed as it rolled across the floor. Saliva poured down his chin. Christy looked away, then felt ashamed for her reaction.

"You're wrong about Granny," Mrs. O'Teale said. "She's got the second sight. Sees signs and portents where you and me just sees clouds or rain or embers in the fire. She's a wise 'un, Granny is. Knows things you and I plumb can't."

"I'm sure she does. But I wish she could give me another chance. Maybe I know one or two things too. Maybe together we could help the children. I've been thinking about Mountie. If I worked with her, took some extra time, we might be able to help her speak."

A glimmer of hope sparked the woman's tired brown eyes then faded. "You had me a-goin' there for a minute. But all the book learnin' in the world ain't a-goin' to fix my Mountie."

"It wouldn't hurt to try, would it?"

Mrs. O'Teale started to answer, but suddenly her mouth

dropped open. There, in the doorway, stood Granny O'Teale, flanked by Mountie, Orter Ball, George, and Thomas. The old woman pointed a shaking finger at Christy, her eyes flaring.

"Out!" she cried. "Out of here, or there'll be the devil to pay, you hear?"

"Granny," Mrs. O'Teale began, "she ain't hurt nobody—"

"What were ya thinkin', Swannie?" Granny demanded. "You gone as simple minded as Wilmer? That girl has a curse on her as black as midnight."

Christy stood. When she reached the doorway, Granny and the children backed away. "Granny," Christy said, trying to keep her voice from revealing the anger she felt. "I came here to make peace with you, to show you that there's nothing to be afraid of." She stepped onto the porch.

Granny stood her ground a few feet away. Mountie clung to her hand, but the other children backed away into the filthy yard.

"I ain't afraid of you," Granny said. "I'm just protectin' what's mine."

"I don't want to harm the children," Christy persisted. "I came here to the Cove to help. To teach. Learning to read and write can't hurt Mountie or Mary or Smith or the others."

"It ain't the learning and such. It's you. You're the one hurt Bob Allen and little Mary. You're the one made the lightning hit."

"Those were accidents, that's all. I can't control the weather."

Granny's eyes narrowed to slits. "How do you explain the raven, then? Surest sign of a curse I heard of in all my days."

Christy glanced back at Mrs. O'Teale. She was standing in the doorway, her face blank. Behind her, Wilmer grunted and drooled. Near Christy's feet, a chicken pecked at what looked like human waste.

Suddenly a feeling of weariness overwhelmed Christy, weighing her down like a great, impossible burden. What was she thinking, standing here in filth and horrible poverty, trying to reason with a frightened old woman? Miss Alice and the doctor had been right. Christy couldn't change generations' worth of ignorance with a few well-chosen words. She'd been a fool to think she had that kind of power. She'd been a fool to think she could leave her comfortable life in Asheville and make a difference here. What did she, Christy Huddleston, have to offer these desperate, unhappy people?

"I just wanted to help, Granny," Christy whispered. Tears came to her eyes, and she wiped them away with the back of her hand.

"Don't need no help from some city gal with a curse on her head," Granny said, but her voice had softened just a touch, as if she sensed that she'd finally won.

"I wish I understood what you're so afraid of," Christy said. She crouched beside Mountie. Granny tugged on the girl's arm, but Mountie didn't budge, and at last Granny gave in.

"Mountie, I just want you to know how much I'll miss you," Christy said. The little girl stared at her, eyes wide and unblinking. Christy reached over and gently pulled Mountie's shabby coat closed. "You take care of yourself, you hear?" She stood and smiled at the other children. "I'll miss all of you," she said.

Granny tightened her grip on Mountie, pulling her close. Miss Alice had said there was good in Granny's heart, good in all of God's children. But perhaps Miss Alice could see what others couldn't. When Christy looked at Granny, all she saw was fear and ignorance and hate.

"All right," Christy said. "All right, Granny. You win."

She ran across the yard to the path. Her long skirt tore on a holly bush, but she didn't stop running until the O'Teale cabin had vanished from sight. She made a wide detour around the dead rabbit.

Halfway to the mission house, Christy heard someone approaching. It was Mary O'Teale, heading home. Christy hid behind a tree until the little girl had passed. She had failed Mary, failed all the children. She didn't want to have to face Mary—not now, not ever again.

Nine

AT THE MISSION HOUSE, CHRISTY DASHED UP THE STAIRS to her bedroom. There she changed all her clothes and brushed her long hair by a wide-open window so that the clean mountain air could pour through it. She washed her face, first in warm water, then in cold, scrubbing her hands over and over. But try as she might, she could not scrub out the memory of what she had seen at the O'Teales' cabin.

Miss Alice, David, Ruby Mae, and Miss Ida were at the dinner table by the time Christy made it downstairs. She felt woozy, but she forced a smile as she sat next to Ruby Mae. Miss Ida passed plates of salmon croquettes and hash-browned potatoes. She was a fine cook, and normally Christy would have enjoyed the food. But tonight her stomach churned.

"I hear you went to the O'Teales'. How did your visit go?" David asked.

Christy reached for her fork and stabbed half-heartedly at the salmon. "Let's just say that Miss Alice and Doctor Mac-Neill were right. It was a waste of time."

"I'm sorry it wasn't what you'd hoped for," Miss Alice said gently.

"Not what I'd hoped—" Christy choked on the words, then caught herself. Her head was spinning. "I'd rather not talk about it."

"I understand," Miss Alice said.

Silence fell over the table. A sullen Ruby Mae stared at her plate.

"Aren't you going to eat, Ruby Mae?" Miss Ida chided. "I can always count on you to take seconds, goodness knows."

"I don't want to be no bundle," Ruby Mae muttered. She glared at Christy, then down at her plate.

"What are you talking about, dear?" Miss Alice asked.

"Don't pay me no mind. I just talk for the sake o' talkin'."

Miss Ida cleared her throat. "I've forgotten my cooked apples," she said, rushing off to the kitchen. A moment later she returned with a steaming bowl. "Here, David," she said. "Your favorite. Lots of cinnamon."

"Well," said Miss Alice, "I'm happy to report that the doctor says Granny's herb concoction is indeed the cause of those mysterious rashes. He treated all the children who were affected. I believe David and I managed to convince them that if they insist on carrying her herb mixture around, they need to put it in a pocket and keep it away from their skin."

"I done tied mine around my waist, see?" Ruby Mae said to Christy, eyeing her angrily.

"She doesn't need to see it. She can smell it," David said. He took a sip of milk. "Don't you understand what nonsense all that superstitious stuff is, Ruby Mae? I'd have hoped to have at least gotten through to you, of all people. After all, you live right here with Christy."

"All the more reason for me to protect myself," Ruby Mae countered, accepting the bowl of apples from David. "Don't know when she might spread the curse to me."

Ruby Mae shoved the apples toward Christy. The steam wafted up toward Christy's face. She swallowed back the sour taste in her mouth.

"I just don't know why we can't get through to you, Ruby Mae!" David declared in exasperation.

"Don't bother, David," Christy said bitterly. "There isn't any point in trying to reach her. There isn't any point in trying to reach any of them—" Suddenly her stomach did a wild flip and she knew she was going to be sick. "Excuse me," she managed to blurt.

She dashed out of the dining room and out into the yard. Moments later she felt Miss Alice's firm, cool hands supporting her head. "Go ahead, Christy," she said. "Get rid of everything. You'll feel better now."

"I—I haven't been so sick since I was a little girl."

"No, don't try to talk."

Finally it was over. Christy stood on unsteady feet. "I . . . I have to go think . . ."

"You go on upstairs," Miss Alice said gently. "I'll come by later and we can talk."

<hr>

Christy sat on her bed, staring bleakly at her lesson plans. When she heard a soft knock on the door, she knew who it was. "Come on in, Miss Alice."

"How are you feeling?" Miss Alice sat down on the edge of the bed.

"All right, physically. But . . ." Christy fought back the tears burning her eyes. "But I'm so confused, Miss Alice. I think maybe Father and Mother were right. Everyone was right, all the people who said I don't belong here. I wasn't willing to listen. I thought I could come here and be welcomed with open arms. I thought I could make a difference." She began to sob. "I . . . I can't fight the ignorance and superstition. I can't."

She cried for several minutes, sobbing while Miss Alice listened quietly. At last Christy lifted her head to look at the peaceful woman. Suddenly she needed to know what Miss Alice was thinking.

"Am I wrong to feel this way?" she asked.

"Any sensitive person would feel exactly as you feel." Miss Alice's voice was matter-of-fact. "Maybe it's just as well all this has happened. Now is as good a time as any to decide whether you'll go home or not—provided you make your decision on a true basis."

"What do you mean 'a true basis'?"

"The way life really is."

"Not much of life can be as bad as what I saw this afternoon," Christy said.

"You'd be surprised. Every bit of life, every single one of us, has a dark side," Miss Alice replied. "When you decided to leave home and take this teaching job, you were leaving the safety and security you'd known all your life. I was the same way. Many of us are. Then we get our first good look at the way life really is, and a lot of us want to run back to shelter in a hurry."

Christy hugged her pillow. "You? Even you?"

"Yes, certainly."

Christy thought of the horrible conditions at the O'Teale

cabin, of Wilmer, of poor Mountie . . . even of the little rabbit that had never had a chance. How could there be such suffering? How could she fight such horrible things?

"But why did you stay?" Christy asked. "When you wanted to leave? When you saw all the evil here?"

Miss Alice considered for a moment. "I believe that you've got to see life the way it really is before you can do anything about evil, Christy. Certainly, people like you are more sensitive than others. But if we're going to work on God's side, we have to decide to open our hearts to the griefs and pain all around us. It's not an easy decision."

"Miss Alice, even if you're right, how can I fight back against the things Granny has said? I can't reach the children if they fear me." Christy gave a bitter laugh. "And I can't be a teacher if I don't have any students."

Miss Alice fell silent for a moment. "I can tell you this. There's a healing power in love, Christy," she said at last. "I've seen it work miracles."

Miss Alice had such peace about her, such a sense of being at home no matter where she was. Christy wanted that feeling, but it seemed as far away as her family and her cozy bedroom back in Asheville.

"I just don't know," Christy whispered at last.

"Know what?"

"If I should stay. If there's any point in it."

Miss Alice nodded, as if she'd asked herself the same question, once upon a time. "First, ask yourself this, Christy: who are you?"

"I wish I knew."

"But you can know. You're important, terribly important.

Each of us is. You're unique. So is David. And Miss Ida. And Ruby Mae and Doctor MacNeill. No one else in all the world can fill David's place or mine or yours. Other teachers may come here to Cutter Gap, but you and you alone have a special gift to offer these people. If you don't do the work that God has given you to do, that work may never be done."

She rose to leave. "It's late and you're tired. But here's something for you to sleep on: Were you supposed to come here, Christy? Or were you just running away from home?"

Christy watched the door close behind Miss Alice. After a while, she retrieved her diary off the dresser. *Was I supposed to come here?* she wondered. She wanted someone to tell her the answer—someone, anyone. But the only person who could answer that question was Christy herself. And she was afraid she already knew the answer.

She opened her diary and scanned the last lines she'd written: *Today braids. Tomorrow the world!*

How hopeful and foolish that sounded now.

Her eyes fell on another passage: *Well, like it or not, Ruby Mae is clearly going to be my bundle.*

Christy groaned. Had Ruby Mae read those words today? That would explain her sullen behavior at the dinner table. She must be feeling terribly hurt and angry. Christy knew she should go to Ruby Mae and explain that she hadn't meant anything when she'd written those words. Certainly the last thing she'd intended to do was to hurt her young student.

She started for the door then stopped herself. What was the point? To begin with, the girl shouldn't have been snooping in her diary. And in any case, Ruby Mae was still wearing Granny's herbs—still apparently convinced Christy was cursed. Why bother trying to console Ruby Mae? There was no point.

Christy realized that she already knew the answer to Miss Alice's question. Tomorrow, she would start packing.

It was time to go home.

Ten

ON SATURDAY MORNING, SOMEONE KNOCKED ON CHRISTY'S door while she was packing. Quickly she set aside the blouse she had been folding. "Come in," she called.

Ruby Mae stuck her head inside the door. "You're sure now?" she said sullenly. "I don't want to be a-steppin' on your privacy or nothin.'"

"Ruby Mae," Christy said, "when I wrote that, I didn't mean that I didn't like having you around. I only meant that sometimes a person wants to be alone. Can you understand that?"

"I just come up 'cause Miz Ida done made me. Said the buckwheat cakes she made are gettin' cold."

"Oh. Would you mind telling her I'm not hungry this morning?"

Ruby Mae put her hands on her hips. "Where's all your things?"

"What— oh, you mean the things on my dresser? I just . . . I was just rearranging." There was no point in telling Ruby

Mae she was packing. If Ruby Mae knew, the entire Cove would know by this afternoon.

"Well, I best be goin'. Don't want to talk your ears plumb off."

Christy ran to Ruby Mae and took her by the arm. Granny's pouch of herbs was still tied around her waist. "Ruby Mae," she said gently, "have you ever said something that just came out wrong? Something that hurt somebody when you didn't mean it to?"

"Sure." Ruby Mae crossed her arms over her chest. "I say the wrong things regular as a clock a-strikin' the hour. You know for yourself I can't keep my mouth shut for more than a minute or two. Dumb things is bound and certain to come out."

The pain in Ruby Mae's voice made Christy wince. Part of her was angry at Ruby Mae, the way she was angry with all the mountain people. After all, this girl was standing in Christy's room, just inches away, wearing a pouch of foul-smelling herbs, just in case Christy was cursed.

And yet, she also felt pity for Ruby Mae, a confused teenager who'd thought she'd found a new friend in Christy. However unintentionally, Christy had repaid that friendship with hurt.

"I have something for you." Christy went to her trunk and pulled out her diary. She opened it and yanked out the first few pages filled with her careful handwriting.

"What in tarnation are you doin'?" Ruby Mae cried.

Christy held out the black leather book. "I want you to have this."

Ruby Mae's eyes went wide. "Oh, no, Miz Christy, I couldn't rightly—"

"Why? Because it's cursed?" Christy demanded, surprised by the bitterness in her own voice.

Slowly Ruby Mae shook her head. "I just . . . It's yours. It's your private book."

"Now it's yours. I want you to write in it every day."

"I ain't no writer. What could the likes of me ever write in a fancy book?"

"Just pretend it's a friend. A friend you can talk to when no one else will listen."

A slow smile dawned on Ruby Mae's face as she accepted the book. "A friend?"

"Maybe you should even give it a name. How about . . . hmm . . . How about Rose? I've always liked that name."

"Rose." Ruby Mae tried the name on for size. "That's a fine name, Miz Christy." She stroked the leather cover tenderly.

"Here. You'll need a pen too. And remember. Whatever you write in there is private. That means you can say anything you want, even if it doesn't always come out just the way you meant it to."

Ruby Mae gave a small nod. "Thank you, Miz Christy."

"Now run and tell Miss Ida I won't be having breakfast."

When she was alone again, Christy scanned the pages she'd ripped from the diary—the chronicle of her magnificent adventure in the mountains. A sentence on the first page caught her attention: *I have begun my great adventure this day, and although things have not gone exactly as I had hoped, I am still committed to my dream of teaching at the mission.*

Well, she was not committed to her dream anymore, that much was certain. She stuffed the pages in her trunk—all except the last one. It was her letter of resignation, the letter she would give to Miss Alice tomorrow, after David's sermon.

She would ask him to accompany her back to the train station at El Pano. Perhaps they could borrow Miss Alice's horse. It would be a long, hard trip, but when it was over, she'd be on her way back home. Home, where she would once again be safe and secure and loved.

⌐#⌐

The service was over. The crowd was gone, the schoolroom deserted. Christy stood in the middle of the room breathing in the now familiar smells of chalk dust, fresh paint, and woodsmoke. She fingered the resignation letter in her skirt pocket. She still hadn't told David or Miss Alice that she planned to leave today. She'd tried to—a hundred times, it seemed—but each time she'd opened her mouth to say the words, a choked sob had come out instead.

Besides, her letter said all that needed to be said:

> *Effective immediately, I will be resigning from my post as teacher at the Cutter Gap mission school. I am deeply sorry that I must leave, but I have determined that I am not suited to the position.*
>
> Sincerely,
Christy Rudd
Huddleston

Not suited to the position. Not suited because she was weak and afraid. Not suited because her stomach revolted at the sight of her students' homes. Not suited because she could not find a way to fight evil and ignorance, not the way someone like Miss Alice could.

She should find David. He was probably down at his bunkhouse. She wanted to tell him first, since David would be easier than Miss Alice. Miss Alice would not be able to hide her disappointment in Christy. Just imagining the look in her eyes made Christy ache inside.

Christy ran her fingers over the worn surface of her desk. It was almost funny, when she thought about it. A silly raven had landed here and changed her life forever.

She turned to leave. Near the door, she spied a ragged brown coat lying on a desk. It was Mountie's. Christy would recognize the shabby, oversized thing anywhere. It was still unseasonably warm out, and it had been hot today during the service. Mountie must have left the coat behind by accident.

Christy touched the dirty brown fabric. It had been patched and repatched a dozen times. All the buttons were missing. How many times had she seen Mountie clutching the lapels to keep out the winter wind?

Poor Mountie. Christy could practically hear the mean chant of the boys at the noon recess, taunting the speechless little girl:

> *Mush-mouthed Millie,*
> *Can't even speak.*
> *Jabber jaybird,*
> *Marbles in the beak.*

Suddenly an idea came to her. At least she could do one small thing before she abandoned Mountie for good.

With the coat in hand, Christy headed for the mission house. Everyone was gone, probably having tea at Miss Alice's cabin. She selected four gold buttons from Miss Ida's sewing box in the kitchen cupboard, along with a needle and thread. One by one, she sewed the buttons onto Mountie's coat. She was just tying the last knot when Ruby Mae appeared at the kitchen door.

"Fine sermon today," she commented, joining Christy at the table. She was still wearing the herb pouch around her waist.

"Yes, David's a wonderful speaker."

"What's that you're up to?"

"Mountie left her coat behind in the schoolroom. I'm just sewing some buttons on it."

Ruby Mae rolled her eyes. "Granny'll like that."

Christy winced. "Oh, no! What was I thinking? She'll probably assume I'm trying to put some kind of curse on Mountie, won't she?" Angrily, she tossed the coat onto the table. "I can't even sew on some buttons without getting into trouble."

With grim determination, Christy found a pair of scissors in Miss Ida's box. She grabbed the coat.

"What are you doin'?" Ruby Mae cried.

"I'm taking off the buttons. Mountie needs this coat. If Granny thinks I've been near it, she won't let Mountie wear it." The horrible unfairness of it all burned in her heart.

Ruby Mae grabbed the scissors. "There's no need for her to know, now, is there? S'posin' I put it back in the school? Anyone asks, I'll say I sewed on the buttons."

"What if the coat is cursed?" Christy challenged. "How do you know it isn't?"

Ruby Mae gave a shrug. "In January—" she smiled— "buttons win out over curses."

Clutching the little coat, Christy followed Ruby Mae outside. As they walked along, the girl chattered away, just like she always did. "You know," she said, "there's somethin' you got to understand, Miz Christy. Granny's just lookin' out for her family."

Christy didn't answer. She had other things on her mind and was only half listening. What if David couldn't take her to the station today? What if Miss Alice refused to accept her resignation?

"I s'pose when school got a-goin'," Ruby Mae was saying, "she sort of felt all left behind. Granny's right partial to Mary and Mountie, 'specially Mountie."

Christy stopped in her tracks as Ruby Mae's words finally began to register. Maybe that was it. Maybe Granny was so afraid of Christy because it meant losing the company of her great-grandchildren.

She touched Ruby Mae's shoulder. "You know, Ruby Mae," she said, "I'm beginning to think I should have listened to you more while I had the chance."

"I don't rightly get what you're aimin' at, Miz Christy."

"Never mind. I'm just sorry, that's all."

She started to hand the coat to Ruby Mae, but a noise coming from the edge of the woods made her pause. It was Granny, with Mary and Mountie, no doubt returning for the missing coat. Granny froze. She scowled at the coat in Christy's hands. But before Granny could say a word, Mountie was dashing over to retrieve the garment.

Christy handed it to her. It took Mountie a moment before she noticed the new buttons. When she did, her little face transformed, her expression becoming a mixture of awe and pure joy. She let out a strange, musical giggle.

"Mountie," Christy asked softly, "what's funny?"

Gleefully, Mountie held up the coat for Mary and Granny to see.

"What have you done to that coat?" Granny snapped.

Mountie tugged on Christy's sleeve.

"What is it, Mountie?" Christy asked.

Mountie screwed her face into a look of pure concentration. "Look at my buttons!" she suddenly blurted. "Look at my buttons!"

Silence fell. A bird chirped from its perch on the mission house roof. Wind rustled the bare-limbed trees.

"Mountie," Christy whispered, "what did you say?"

"Teacher, look! Look at my buttons! See how pretty?"

Christy blinked in disbelief at the beautiful words coming from the little girl's mouth. They were a little slurred, perhaps, but to Christy they sounded as clear and joyful as the peals of a church bell.

"Did you hear what I heard?" she asked Ruby Mae.

Ruby Mae nodded, eyes wide. "I'm as plumb mystified as you, Miz Christy."

Christy looked over at Granny. Even from a distance, she could tell that the old woman had tears in her eyes. Mary wore a smile so big it seemed to take up her whole face.

Mountie grabbed Christy's hand. "Teacher! See them?"

Christy knelt down. "I see them, Mountie."

Mary broke free of Granny and ran over to hug her big sister.

"See my buttons, Mary?" Mountie said.

"I see 'em. They's shiny as real gold. And I heard you, all the ways over there, Mountie!" Mary smiled shyly at Christy. "Thank you, Miz Christy," she whispered. "You done a good thing, I reckon."

She had done a good thing. A small thing, yes. But a thing that might help change Mountie's life.

What if Mountie was part of God's plan for Christy? Part of the work, as Miss Alice had said, that only Christy could do? What if she had left yesterday, and those buttons had remained forever in Miss Ida's sewing box?

If Christy left Cutter Gap now, superstition and ignorance would have triumphed. If she stayed, maybe there would be other Mounties—other small miracles.

Christy reached into her pocket and slowly crumpled her resignation letter.

"Come on, girls," Granny called. "Get away from her."

"I just want you to know something, Granny," Christy said, moving closer. "I'm staying. I almost left because of you and the things you've been saying about me. But I'm staying. And nothing you can say will change my mind. I'm staying because I care about Mountie and Mary and the rest of these children." She paused and smiled, remembering what Ruby Mae had said about Granny. "Just like you do."

Granny worked her mouth, as if she were searching for words.

Mountie rushed over to her. "Granny, see my buttons?"

Granny squeezed the girl's hand. "I see, child." She looked over at Christy.

For the first time, Christy thought she saw something more than fear and anger there—maybe even a glimmer of respect.

But after a long moment, Granny turned away without another word, pulling Mountie along.

Mary turned back to Christy. "Thank you," she whispered again, and then she, too, was gone.

Eleven

On Monday morning, Christy made her way over the plank walk across the muddy school yard. She clutched her lesson plan to her chest. She'd worked on it all last evening, although she wasn't sure why. How many children would even come today? Ten? Five? None?

Miss Alice and David had told her to keep showing up every day, no matter what. Eventually, they said, she'd have her students back. She hadn't told them about her resignation letter. It was still crumpled in her pocket.

Inside the schoolroom, a fire already burned in the old stove. David had come in earlier to start it, although it was still strangely warm outside. Christy took the ball of paper out of her pocket and tossed it into the potbellied stove. It was a satisfying feeling, watching it crackle and burn, then vanish.

She went to her desk and set down her lesson book. She turned to the last roll call. Just a handful of students. She'd never have dreamed she'd miss having all sixty-seven of them, but she did.

As she started to sit, she noticed a familiar book lying

open on her chair. It was her diary. She picked it up, smiling at the childish scrawl, marred by cross outs. It filled the page in huge letters, too big to ignore:

Miz Cristy is right trubling sometimz. She'z alwayz makin me wash my fas and brush the mous nests outa my har. And she gits thez feraway looks in her eyz sometimz. Won't listn a-tall. Still and all even if shez fer shure cursd, I'm prowd and onered to call her my frend.

"Ain't you never heard of a thing called privacy?"

Christy jumped, nearly dropping the diary. "Ruby Mae! I was just—"

Ruby Mae stood in the doorway, tapping her foot. "Just readin' my Rose, I'm a-guessin."

"I apologize, really I do. It's just that it was sitting right there, in my chair, where I could hardly miss it—"

"Imagine that." Ruby Mae grinned. "Wonder how it got there?"

Christy closed the diary and passed it to Ruby Mae. "I'm proud and honored to call you my friend too," she said softly.

Ruby Mae blushed and went quickly to one of the windows. Christy was surprised to see that she was no longer wearing Granny's herbs.

"Ruby Mae," Christy said, "do you think anyone will show up today?"

"Ain't you looked outside?"

Christy joined her at the window. Coming up the hill she saw Lundy Taylor and Wraight Holt, trailed by several others. "The Holts are coming!" she exclaimed. "And there's Isaak McHone!"

"Yes'm. I reckon you'll have your hands full today. Everybody's a-comin'."

"But why? Why are they all coming back?"

Ruby Mae rolled her eyes. "It's a good thing you got me to keep you up on Cove gossip, Miz Christy. Don't you even know that Granny says you're uncursed?"

"Uncursed?"

"Yes'm. As of yesterday. Everybody knows."

"Except me. The one who's cursed." Christy narrowed her eyes. "I don't believe it. You're telling me Granny changed her mind about me? How is that possible?"

"Don't rightly know. All I knows is she says she saw a sign yesterday."

"A sign," Christy repeated, torn between laughing and groaning and crying.

Just then she saw two little girls appear out of the dark woods. An old woman with a cane followed behind.

"It's Mountie and Mary," Christy whispered. "They're back. They're all coming back!" She hugged Ruby Mae until the girl pulled away, gasping for breath.

"Watch out for my braids, now," Ruby Mae scolded. "You know it done took me half the night to get 'em just so."

Granny paused at the edge of the schoolyard as Mary and Mountie dashed ahead. The old woman met Christy's eyes and gave a small nod.

"So Granny saw a sign," Christy said. "I wonder what it was?"

"Search me. But I heard it had something to do with four golden coins that fell from heaven."

Christy looked at Ruby Mae. Ruby Mae looked back with a sly grin. "Can't imagine what she meant, Miz Christy," she said. "Can you?"

About Catherine Marshall

Catherine Marshall LeSourd (1914–1983), a *New York Times* bestselling author, is best known for her novel *Christy*. Based on the life of her mother, a teacher of mountain children in poverty-stricken Tennessee, *Christy* captured the hearts of millions and became a popular CBS television series. As her mother reminisced around the kitchen table at Evergreen Farm, Catherine probed for details and insights into the rugged lives of these Appalachian highlanders.

The Christy® of Cutter Gap series, based on the characters of the beloved novel, contains expanded adventures filled with romance, excitement, and intrigue.

Catherine also wrote *Julie*, a sweeping novel of love and adventure, courage and commitment, tragedy and triumph, in a Pennsylvania steel town during the Great Depression.

Catherine's first husband, Peter Marshall, was Chaplain of the U.S. Senate, and her intimate biography of him, *A Man Called Peter*, became an international bestseller and Academy Award Nominated movie. The story shares the power of this dynamic man's love for his God and for the woman he married.

A beloved inspirational writer and speaker, Catherine's enduring career spanned four decades and six continents, and reached over 30 million readers.

CHRISTY'S ADVENTURES CONTINUE IN...

Headstrong and independent, Christy is determined to change the lives of the children in Cutter Gap. Apparently, Christy has angered someone enough to cause a string of mysterious pranks.

Miss Alice warns Christy to be careful as the pranks soon become threatening. What will Christy do when one of her own students turns against her?